T0356463

Live Fast

Live
Fast

A novel

Brigitte Giraud

Translated from the French
by Cory Stockwell

ecco

An Imprint of HarperCollins*Publishers*

LIVE FAST. Copyright © 2025 by Brigitte Giraud. English translation copyright © 2025 by Cory Stockwell. All rights reserved. Printed in the United States of America. No part of this book may be used or reproduced in any manner whatsoever without written permission except in the case of brief quotations embodied in critical articles and reviews. For information, address HarperCollins Publishers, 195 Broadway, New York, NY 10007.

HarperCollins books may be purchased for educational, business, or sales promotional use. For information, please email the Special Markets Department at SPsales@harpercollins.com.

Ecco® and HarperCollins® are trademarks of HarperCollins Publishers.

Originally published as *Vivre Vite* in France in 2022 by Flammarion.

FIRST EDITION

Designed by Patrick Barry

Library of Congress Cataloging-in-Publication Data has been applied for.

ISBN 978-0-06-334672-7

24 25 26 27 28 LBC 5 4 3 2 1

To Théo

Writing means being led to the one place
you'd like to avoid.
—PATRICK AUTRÉAUX

Live Fast

Prologue

AFTER MANY LONG MONTHS OF RESISTING THE daily onslaught of developers urging me to sell the property, I finally gave in.

Today I signed over the house.

When I say the house, I mean the house I bought with Claude twenty years ago, which he never lived in.

Because of the accident. Because of that June day when he accelerated down a city boulevard on a motorcycle that wasn't his. Inspired by Lou Reed, perhaps, who had written "Live fast, die young," stuff like that, in the book Claude was reading at the time, which I found lying on the parquet floor, at the foot of the bed. And which I began to flip through the following night. *Be bad. Get messy.*

I sold my soul, and maybe his as well.

The developer has already bought several plots, including the neighbor's, on which he plans to put up a building that will tower over the yard, that will look down on my privacy from a height of four stories, that will block out the sun. No more silence, no more light. The nature that surrounds me will turn to concrete and the landscape will disappear. On the other side, they're planning to turn the little lane into a proper road that will go right past my house, all to provide access to the new residential area. The birdsong will be drowned out by engine noise. Bulldozers will raze what was once alive.

WHEN CLAUDE AND I bought the property in 1999, the year when France was switching from francs to euros (which meant we had to use the rule of three for even the most minor calculations, as though we were children), the zoning regulations indicated that the house was in a *green zone*—in other words, no construction was allowed in the area. The owner of the house next door told us that you couldn't even cut down a tree, and if you did you'd have to replace it. Every square inch of nature was sacred. That's why we were drawn to this place: we'd be able to live hidden away on the edge of town. There was a cherry tree right outside the window, a maple (a storm uprooted it the year I returned to Algeria), and an Atlas cedar, whose resin, I recently learned, was once used to embalm mummies.

I planted a few more trees, and some others have popped up on their own, like the fig tree that moved in along the back wall. Each one has a story. But Claude didn't see any of this. He only had time to visit: he whistled enthusiastically as he determined how much work had to be done, and figured out a place where he could put his motorcycle. He had just enough time to measure the surface areas, to imagine himself moving about in the space by making a few hand gestures in the air, to sign the documents at the notary's office, to make sarcastic comments in the Crédit Mutuel as he divided the percentage of the loan insurance between us. The place had great potential, as the real-estate jargon goes. We were excited by the prospect of renovating. We'd be able to listen to loud music without bothering the tree-counting neighbor, whose vast lot stretched out behind a natural hedge. We'd be able to stop living out of our suitcases once and for all, and start building our castles in the air.

I moved in alone with our son in the midst of a brutal chronological sequence. Signature of deed of sale. Accident. Move. Funeral.

It was the craziest acceleration of my life. Like being on a roller coaster, hair blowing in the wind, the car on the verge of coming off the rails.

I'm writing from this remote setting where I've landed, and from which I perceive the world as a slightly blurry film that for a long time has been shot without me.

THE HOUSE BECAME THE witness to my life without Claude. A carcass I had to learn to live in, whose partitions I knocked down with great blows of a sledgehammer at the height of my anger. It was a slightly rickety house, and the lot (which we'd hoped to turn into a yard) needed clearing. I felt like I wasn't so much renovating as smashing, ransacking, declaring war on anything that resisted me—plaster, stone, wood—materials I could make martyrs of without anyone throwing me in jail. It was my little revenge against destiny, kicking in the sheet metal of a swinging door, shearing through a filthy burlap cloth, smashing windows as I screamed.

All the while trying to conserve a cocoon in the midst of the chaos so our son could sleep in safety. A brightly colored little burrow with down comforters and pillows, drawings hanging above the bed, and a thick carpet—a rampart against fear and all the ghosts in the night.

AS THE YEARS WENT by, I came to tame this house that I'd initially disliked. At first I lived there as a sleepwalker, mixing up my mornings and evenings, until finally I stopped banging into the walls and started repainting them. No more massacring partitions and drop ceilings, no more considering every square foot an enemy power. I calmed my fury and decided to disguise myself as a respectable person. I had to return to the land of the living. I'd shoot daggers at anyone who said I was a widow. Overwhelmed with grief, yes, but not a widow.

BUT I STILL HAD to grapple with the weeds invading the garden. For months I pulled them out compulsively, in repetitive and disturbing movements, learning their names—couch grass, stinging nettle, purslane—and setting them alight in secret bonfires under the cover of night (lighting fires wasn't allowed because of the fine particles). I got rid of invasive plants like ragweed and ivy that crawled in the shadows, and tracking down these undesirables allowed me to clear my mind at the same time as I cleared the plot.

LITTLE BY LITTLE, I began to reside on the premises in the most bourgeois of ways, as required by one of the clauses in the insurance contract I'd taken out to protect us in case of fire, water damage, or burglary (one misfortune never prevents another, according to Murphy's famous law, which hadn't escaped my notice). I became less enraged and managed to draw up the plans for both floors just as Claude and I had imagined. I knew exactly what he'd have wanted, which materials he'd been considering, as I browsed the pages we'd dog-eared in the Lapeyre catalog. Little by little I recovered my bearings. I met craftsmen who could come pour a slab, change a beam, or tile a damaged floor. Who'd redo the bathroom or install central heating. Maybe one day I'd even feel like taking a bath again.

From time to time I've taken pleasure in choosing a color, matching paint with the wood of a door. I've found beauty in the way low-angled light entered the kitchen just before dinner.

But I didn't understand who the light was for. I preferred rainy days, which at least didn't try to distract me from my sadness. I decided that the house would be what connected me to Claude. What would give a framework to this new life that our son and I hadn't chosen. He was still *our* son, but I'd have to learn to say *my* son. Just as I'd have to give up the *we* that had supported me and learn to say

I. Even though this *I* would flay me by expressing an unwanted solitude and a twisted truth.

I kept the idea of building the little recording studio Claude had wanted for so long. A soundproof room where he'd hoped to be able to work in isolation. It would have contained all the instruments he owned: a bass, a guitar, and the synthesizer he'd just bought (a Sequential Circuits Six-Trak—I'm being precise because it's important in what follows), whose keys he tapped away on while wearing headphones.

I was making slow but steady progress, though it would take me almost twenty years to be done with all the rooms, all the surfaces; it was only last year that I changed the windows. I've just repainted the shutters. If only I'd known I was going to all this trouble just for a developer to raze it all to the ground. I never did get the facade restored—it's still in its slightly dirty original state. It was too expensive. As for the wooden deck we'd planned, I never had it installed. I guess that was the right call.

BUT NONE OF THAT mattered. There was only one thing I was truly obsessed with, and I'd kept it secret so as not to frighten those around me. I didn't talk about it, or rather, I'd stopped talking about it, because after two or three years, it would have seemed suspicious if I'd persisted in trying to understand how the accident happened. An accident whose cause had never been clarified, which meant that my brain had never stopped running wild.

It had taken me all this time to find out whether this

word, *destiny*, which I heard people say here and there, had any meaning. And so now, at the very moment when I'm forced to leave the house so a road can be built, I have to go over it one last time—only this will allow me to finally close the investigation. It's really incredible, since after all Claude died on a road, that a road is being laid down right on top of me. A road, at a time when the planet is dying from all these roads that accelerate carbon dioxide emissions. Claude would have laughed at the irony. That book he was reading, the one by the American rock critic Lester Bangs that I spotted at the foot of the bed, and where I found the quotation from Lou Reed (first attributed to James Dean), is called *Psychotic Reactions and Carburetor Dung*. A story about carburetors—there's just no escaping it.

I'M GOING TO TAKE one last look around the whole thing, just as an owner takes one last look around the house before closing the door for good. Because the house is at the heart of what caused the accident.

If only I hadn't wanted to sell the apartment.

If only I hadn't insisted on visiting that house.

If only my grandfather hadn't committed suicide at the very moment when we needed money.

If only we hadn't received the keys to the house in advance.

If only my mother hadn't called my brother to tell him we had a garage.

If only my brother hadn't parked his motorcycle there during the week he was on vacation.

If only I'd allowed our son to go on vacation with my brother.

If only I hadn't changed the date of my trip to Paris to see my publisher.

If only I'd phoned Claude on the evening of June 21 instead of listening to Hélène tell me about her new relationship.

If only I'd had a cell phone.

If only mommy time hadn't also been daddy time.

If only Stephen King had died in the terrible accident he had three days before Claude's accident.

If only it had rained.

If only Claude had listened to "Don't Panic" by Coldplay, and not "Dirge" by Death in Vegas, before leaving the office.

If only Claude hadn't forgotten his three hundred francs in the bank machine.

If only Denis R. hadn't decided to bring the Citroën 2CV to his father.

IF ONLY THE DAYS preceding the accident hadn't gotten wrapped up in a chain of events that were as inexplicable as they were unexpected.

AND ABOVE ALL, WHY did Tadao Baba, that over-enthusiastic Japanese engineer who revolutionized Honda's history, force his way into my existence, even though he lives six thousand miles away?

WHY WAS THE HONDA CBR900 Fireblade, jewel of the Japanese motorcycle industry, which Claude was riding on

June 22, 1999, authorized for export to Europe but banned in Japan, where it was considered too dangerous?

I'M REVISITING THIS LITANY of ifs that has obsessed me for so many years. And that has made me live my life in the past conditional.

WHEN THERE AREN'T ANY looming catastrophes, you just keep going without turning back: you look straight ahead and move toward the horizon. When a tragic event takes place, you retrace your steps and return to the site of the accident so that you can reenact the whole thing. You try to understand the starting point of every movement, every decision. You rewind and then you rewind again. You become a specialist in causal relationships. You hunt down clues, dissect them, and conduct postmortems. You want to know all there is to know about human nature, about the individual and collective springs from which events gush forth. You can't tell if you're a sociologist, a cop, or a writer. You go mad—you want to understand how it's possible to become a mere statistic, a footnote in the grand scheme of things. When all this time you thought you were unique and immortal.

If Only . . .

1

If only I hadn't wanted to sell the apartment

EVER SINCE THE DAY WE MET, IN A SUBURB OF LYON called Rillieux-la-Pape (it's not as well known as Vaulx-en-Velin, where they've set a lot more cars on fire over the past few decades), Claude and I did everything we could to leave and move to the center of Lyon.

I really enjoyed that time, when I would look through the classifieds to try to find the apartment of our dreams. We fantasized about neighborhoods that were starting to buzz, full of the cafés, cinemas, and shops that were lacking in our working-class suburb. We wanted the opposite of the run-down bedroom community where we'd grown up, something other than those endless straight lines of identical concrete housing blocks.

I FOUND A PLACE to rent without too much difficulty (this was the beginning of the eighties, after all), a big and dingy space that enticed us with its ridiculously low rent (four hundred francs a month—I still have the receipts) and the two very kitschy stucco pillars that made the living room look like an ersatz palace, along with an oak floor that had seen better days. It was time to move on from the linoleum that had been our staple and the in-floor heating that made our mothers' legs swell. We were so amazed our application had been accepted that we didn't even notice the absence of radiators, the unsealed windows, and the fact that the building across from us (it was only fifteen feet away) was an hourly-rate hotel that blocked out the sun.

We were the first of our gang of suburbanites to migrate downtown and land our holy grail: an apartment that could serve as a base, big enough to have friends over and close to the Hôtel-de-Ville subway station. In other words, an ideal spot for parties and impromptu concerts, or to put up anyone who needed to spend the night.

BUT OUR LUCK QUICKLY ran out.

We were soon evicted as a result of gentrification, which would shape our entire path as a couple, though we didn't even know the word at the time. The developer who bought the building with a view to upgrading the apartments offered us a new flat, as required by law, but it was in Vénissieux, another far-flung area well known for its wild nights and its fifteen-floor apartment blocks, which the municipality would soon earmark for demolition. We didn't see ourselves going back to the boonies, no matter how much fate seemed to conspire against us, and so we did whatever was necessary to stay downtown.

AFTER ANOTHER UNSCRUPULOUS LANDLORD forced us out of an apartment near the river, we found out that my grandfather had committed suicide—not to suggest, contrary to how this might sound, that the events are related. What they have in common, if we pan out for a moment, is that my maternal grandfather, a perfect example of the rural exodus of the fifties that brought people to the Lyon urban area, had moved with his family into a little house on the banks of the Rhône, in the Saint-Fons district—the very place where the pharmaceutical firm Rhône-Poulenc, which at the time was running at full speed (it has since been purchased by Sanofi-Aventis), wanted to expand its headquarters. A few years later, my grandparents had to make way for the bulldozers, and they ended up at the bottom of the Vénissieux Towers, which were reserved for all those people who were cut off from their homelands (whether that meant Algeria, Morocco, Portugal, or Auvergne) and who didn't dare to complain about breathing air that was saturated with hydrogen sulfide emitted by the nearby Feyzin refinery. After the death of my grandmother, who no longer knew where to hang her laundry because of the smell of rotten eggs that would permeate the fabric, and who contracted leukemia at an unusually young age after other twists and turns that would be too arduous to deal with here, my grandfather threw himself into the Rhône. They found his body and his identity documents at the Pierre-Bénite dam, in the very heart of what the locals call the petrochemical valley.

WAS IT BECAUSE OF these determining factors, and the inheritance money I received from my mother, that Claude and I became homeowners? Was it so that we could never be evicted again? Maybe we wanted to defuse the situation, and defuse something else as well, a worry we weren't even aware of, one that, for Claude, was fed by a sense of exile, since at the age of four he'd been put on a boat coming from Algeria, a country he'd never see again.

WITHOUT A DOUBT, BECOMING a homeowner is more than just the ideological symbol we think it is.

We bought an apartment in the Croix-Rousse neighborhood from the Boubeker family, who left because they were expecting another baby. We stayed there for ten years, and we spent almost the entire time renovating. This was just what people in our generation did, people in their thirties who were buying and transforming what in Lyon are known as *canuts*, silk workshops built in the nineteenth century with generous ceiling height so that weaving looms could be installed and workers would have a place to sleep. The neighborhood had changed since then, but still retained its share of workers and immigrants. Those of us who were buying wanted to overhaul the spaces—sand, repaint, install open-plan kitchens, and remove the lattice ceilings that owners had put up in the mid-twentieth century to hide the thick wooden beams that were unfashionable in the postwar years.

Now they were back in style. Everyone was talking about authenticity, and the thing to do in the eighties was to expose the beams and the stonework. So that's what Claude and I did, even though it meant spending our weekends in a slightly euphoric state, high on the stain we applied in copious amounts to all the wood surfaces. We listened to Nirvana in our overalls, perched on the little scaffold we'd rented from the hardware store, and felt the joy of owning our own home for the first time. We believed in beauty, convinced we were going to change the place into a temple of good taste. We were in love, and the path before us was wide open.

OUR SON WAS BORN, which raised our energy to levels we hadn't dreamed of. He slept in the only bedroom, where we'd redone the wallpaper, while we slept in the loft, like they used to do in the silk workshops. It's what everyone in the neighborhood did—we all found it romantic to climb up and down the ladder, even when we had to piss at three in the morning. We felt like we were in on a secret, like we knew how to really live. We were cool, confident, and self-assured. I can confirm that it was the perfect life. It lasted ten years.

I DON'T KNOW WHY I ever decided to mess with that equilibrium.

Because I was the one who wanted to leave. I wanted to

move, to start again from scratch. To ratchet up to a new level of coolness. And to aim for perfection itself while I was at it.

So I complained about the ladder we had to deal with in the middle of the night, the lack of intimacy, the extra bedroom we'd need if we had the second child we'd been dreaming about.

And this was when I first began to write, in this interval, this period of dormancy that was also a moment of doubt, since I thought we were missing something important in our lives.

2

If only my grandfather hadn't committed suicide

THERE'S NO CHRONOLOGICAL OR METHODOLOGICAL order to any series of events. Only waves that take shape on the horizon, visible in the ridges they form, little waves or curls that are usually harmless because they're predictable. But there are also groundswells that you don't see coming, tidal waves that rise up and engulf you when you have your back turned.

MAYBE MY GRANDFATHER'S DEATH has nothing to do with any of this. To all appearances, all that came out of it was a sum of money. But you have to know how to use money, to do something with it without losing it. And there's nothing better to do with cash than to put it into real estate. After all, the social class I belong to doesn't understand anything about financial management and avoids it like the plague—best to just convert your windfall into something solid. I may be exaggerating when I use the word *windfall*, since we're talking about a modest sum of money. But it seemed like more than it was because my mother, careful not to meddle with her inheritance tax, transferred it to us all at once.

IN SHORT, THIS MONEY that my mother gave in equal parts to her two children was the exact amount we needed to make a hefty down payment, without which Claude and I wouldn't have been able to take the plunge. Prior to that, for all the good reasons we had to buy—we wanted to build a foundation for our life as a couple, and we didn't want to be evicted anymore—we were still lacking the means.

If my grandfather hadn't put an early end to his days, we wouldn't even have been able to think about buying the apartment, not to mention selling it later to buy something else. Which means we'd never have set foot in that vast house that would end up being the source of the accident, even if we'd had all the time in the world.

BUT MY GRANDFATHER ISN'T the only cause of this money that fell into our laps, so to speak. The other source of funds, and without a doubt the more important of the two, was the real-estate speculation that began to turn heads at the end of the eighties. You buy for 320,000 francs, and ten years later you sell for double. Jackpot. We were surrounded by crafty devils talking about it nonstop, and even though we pretended we weren't like that, we ended up getting out the calculator and chatting about what the price per square foot would be after we renovated. We were very tempted by the prospect of "making a killing" (there was no shortage of expressions to refer to the "amazing deals" that people everywhere— including our left-wing friends—were making, without the slightest scruple). And even if we were doing just fine in the loft of our little silk workshop, we ended up being won over by what felt like a need to expand and make easy money.

Except that even if we were going to make a lot of money, we'd also have to spend a lot of money. Which made for a challenge we found exciting—I'd be lying if I said otherwise.

CLAUDE GAVE ME FREE rein, with all the gentleness and casualness that made him who he was. As long as I had the energy to resell the apartment and start from scratch. *Why not?* It was what he said when he wasn't opposed to something. *Why not?*

He'd listen to Oasis and tell me about the squabble between the Gallagher brothers, the singer Liam and the guitarist Noel. During the evening he'd turn up the volume in the kitchen, where the CD player was, and where he introduced me to the soundtrack of the era. Blur or Oasis? Just like the previous generation had asked: Rolling Stones or Beatles? It was these questions that really got him worked up. More than exposed stone walls or castles in the sky. Even though he was good with his tools, and loved doing work with his miter box. *Why not?*

I DEVOTED ENTIRE DAYS to my search. I had no idea that I was putting our life in danger. I needed to keep moving. At the same time as I was writing what would become my first novel (the story of a man locked away in prison because he'd killed his father), I scanned the classifieds, made calls, tallied our expenses, and scheduled viewings of our apartment. What began as a mere idea, a little diversion, had become something I urgently needed to do. Adrenaline had me in its grip. I waited for the 69, a local classified ads newspaper, to be dropped in our mailbox on Mondays (this was just before the internet); I made appointments, and I looked for the ideal home, which I imagined to be a house with a yard. I don't know where I got the sudden desire to get my hands dirty, plant hydrangeas (I'd seen lots of them during our vacation in Brittany), eat breakfast outside, invite friends over, and have a place where our son could play outdoors. I was looking for an old house with plenty of south-facing windows, three or four bedrooms (we needed space for all Claude's instruments, and I was also imagining an office for myself), a little yard or a patio, and a place to park the motorcycle. I was aiming for the impossible, in other words. Maybe that's what attracted me.

I SPENT MY TIME visiting and waiting—my whole life revolved around the gem I was going to discover. Big, bright, comfortable. I visited, and I wrote. Was there some secret link between these two needs? Probably the impossibility of keeping still, even though I worked in an office two days a week.

I ENDED UP BECOMING an expert in apartment hunting. Nobody deciphered ads like me—I could spot drawbacks in the way they were written. I loved this language of hidden traps and omissions that turned me into an interpreter, a sly dog you didn't mess with.

There should have been a little voice telling me to stay put, not to leave our refurbished silk workshop, which was a tight fit, sure, a bit spartan, but where we managed perfectly well. There should have been a little voice tying me to my chair on Saturday when I went house hunting while Claude worked.

Stay put.

There was still time to bring it all to a halt. I hadn't committed to anything with a bank or a real-estate agency. I was free, and everything was going fine.

But I'm not the kind of person who gives up.

A hideous phrase, but that hasn't stopped me from writing it.

I even stepped things up, putting little notes in the mailboxes of all the houses on or near our street. I told myself that a town house would be ideal. Claude acquiesced—sure, *why not*, whatever makes you happy. His only wish, the only thing he wanted, was to be high up, on a hill, so he could sit on the balcony and look out at the roofs while he smoked. Was this the distant echo, the hidden memory, of that patio in Algiers where he'd ridden his tricycle when he was a kid? Of that open sky where from time to time the echo of detonations would reverberate? As for me, I preferred to be lower. On solid ground. I remember that urge, which would later come to seem suspicious. That desire that became an obsession.

3

If only I hadn't visited that house

A CLASSIFIED AD LURED ME TOWARD A HOUSE THAT was nearby, just a few streets away from our own. I went with our son, who was already seven. I knew it was too expensive, far too expensive for us. I went purely out of curiosity, as they say, to see what was hidden behind that high wall along which we often walked.

I was shocked—completely dazzled. All at once I threw my list of requirements out the window. This was the place. It had to be here. But we didn't have the money. I remember all that green, the big trees and the swings. I remember the peonies swaying on their stems. The inside was dark and charming. The wooden staircase, with its shiny handrail, made a quarter turn as it ascended, and creaked under my weight. There were four bedrooms upstairs, all with wallpaper from another era, and a charming old bathroom.

Walking around the enormous yard, examining the

shed near the back fence, I literally choked with regret, because it was clear that this house and its surrounding property weren't going to be ours. But then I noticed that there was another house in a hidden corner behind the hedge, a smaller and more modest house, paint flaking on its closed shutters—an abandoned house disappearing into the vegetation.

THAT'S WHEN I SHOULD have shut my mouth.

AN ABANDONED HOUSE THAT I noticed in a blind spot, like those ruins people sometimes discover buried under the brush at the edge of a forest, probably haunted, oozing moisture, saltpeter, and a macabre history. Or those buildings that have been clumsily boarded up, that still hold within them the fear of stormy nights, half-burned logs in the fireplace, broken glass and old papers strewn across the floor.

ALL OF WHICH DETERS most normal people.

I COULDN'T HELP MYSELF. I inquired.

THE WOMAN TOLD ME that house belonged to her brother and he wasn't interested in selling. She gave the impression that there was some link to the war: the Resistance hero Jean Moulin had held secret meetings there. I forgot to mention that we were in the village of Caluire, which adjoins the fourth arrondissement of Lyon, Caluire-et-Cuire, the city where Jean Moulin was arrested. She told me a story of English paratroopers that his family supposedly hid in the basement, of weapons buried at the back of the yard. She pointed vaguely toward the earth beneath a conifer (I later found out that it was an Atlas cedar). She also brought up the ammunition that her parents hid in her crib when she was a baby, and the bars of soap that the family stockpiled to make explosives. Her brother lived in Nice, and he wasn't selling. No, there was no use insisting.

ANYONE ELSE WOULD HAVE turned away and fled that house, which was no doubt full of evil spirits. Anyone else would have left it all alone with its past.

I did the opposite, under the spell of its enigma and two impossible tasks: buying the house and finding the weapons hidden in the yard. As though the adventure would turn me into a resistance fighter. It was totally unexpected, which may be why I had no inkling of the chain of events that was about to turn our lives upside down.

JUST A FEW DAYS later (I couldn't help myself), I wrote a letter to Madame Mercier, that was the woman's name, telling her how much I'd loved the place, how attached I was to the neighborhood, things I thought might make her brother change his mind. The faraway stubborn brother. It felt like they were in on it together, like they had some kind of secret.

THEN I WAITED, AND I still feel ashamed that I did.

I DIDN'T GET ANY response to my letter. It was naive to think that two strangers would allow themselves to be affected by the feelings of a young woman looking for somewhere to live. I kept waiting. I was disappointed, but also a little offended that these bourgeois Merciers would resist my entreaty.

I SHOULD HAVE SEEN it as a sign. I should have blessed them instead of hoping to convince them. Instead of making the whole thing about more than just house hunting. If I were simplistic, I'd call it a latent form of class struggle. Well, let's just say I'm an enlightened simpleton.

I KEPT LOOKING. AFTER all, I had my whole life in front of me, or at least that's what I thought. Everything was going fine, so I stopped thinking about it. There'd be other opportunities. I kept skimming the classifieds and chasing up the real-estate agencies. I didn't really mind this nonstop searching—it added a bit of spice to my daily grind.

I didn't know whether it was better to sell first or buy first. I heard a lot of talk about bridge loans, and thought about the sleepless nights that would ensue if we took one out. The one thing I was sure of was that nothing could keep me from getting what I wanted. I learned all about interest rates and banking terms. I was relentless, marching forth with a level of energy I've never had since. When I look back, I see myself as a little one-woman army, at once captain, foot soldier, and gunner.

ONE DAY I VISITED a big apartment that oozed charm, also in Caluire, but a little farther out, near the public swimming pool, at the edge of the Montessuy high-rises, which was perhaps more our style after all. Life seemed different there, slower. Our son would have to change schools, which wouldn't be a huge deal. This apartment, with its shared courtyard, somehow felt really peaceful; it was large, which would allow us to spread out a bit and work on our creative projects; we might even be able to rent a room out to a student. We'd have to find a garage, but we could think about that later.

WE STAYED UP LATE debating the pros and cons. Advantages and disadvantages. Desires and concerns. Additions and subtractions. And these difficult choices gave rise to tensions. All Claude and I talked about was my desire to move, this desire that haunted me, that left no time for anything else, and that made me frantic, sometimes ridiculously so. I went back to see the apartment in Montessuy with my friend Marie because I wanted someone else's opinion. The apartment was built on the slope of a wooded hill overlooking the Rhône, and on that day there were rabbits on the property. It seemed like a sign, the kind of argument that couldn't have been dreamed up by any real-estate agent (this was also the time when I was learning all about this tribe, with their predictable jargon, their tight shirts, and their depressive tendencies).

CLAUDE VISITED THE APARTMENT some time later, and found that it had its charms, despite its distance from any cafés or cinemas, not to mention offices of the newspaper where he worked. And since he was starting to get sick of my endless search, he said it was fine. He was the opposite of me: all he needed was a place to sleep, listen to music, and park his motorcycle. He wasn't consumed by a need for perfection. The only thing that bothered him was not living close to the Mediterranean. He didn't like it when summer turned to fall, when shorter days meant colder temperatures. In fact it was mostly the passing of time that worried him, the years going by—he had just turned forty, after all. Easygoing as he was about the apartment, the arrival of November really made him suffer. And that's an understatement.

NOVEMBER WAS HERE, AND we were about to sign the preliminary sales agreement. Claude and I were both excited about how this change was going to bring a little movement to our lives. Buying such a spacious apartment was a real event. I'd turn one of the rooms into an office, we'd have a spare bedroom, Claude could fix things up here and there, and he'd also be able to rehearse with his band in the storage building at the back of the shared courtyard, as long as the homeowners' association was OK with it. We'd become members at the pool, which would do us a lot of good. We just had to stay positive.

We still had to sell our little silk workshop. I'd organize viewings, make sure the place was clean, put tulips in a vase on the kitchen table, and keep our son from spreading his toys all over the apartment. We'd avoid hanging our laundry in the middle of the living room, polish the bathroom and the stove after every use, and make sure there were no guitars blocking the hallways.

AND THAT'S WHEN MADAME Mercier called.

WHEN I LOOK BACK now, it seems like it was the devil himself who was calling. And yet the name Mercier contains the word *merci*. I should have said "Non merci."

She called on the landline (it's hard to remember that world without cell phones) one rainy evening to tell us her brother had changed his mind. He was willing to sell us the ruin of a house I'd been dreaming about night and day, and for which I'd made a ridiculously high offer. The stupid brother wasn't so stupid after all—he'd just been waiting for some harebrained woman to come along and beg him to part ways with this house that was barely standing.

But it was too late, because we'd already committed to something else. The house was no longer an option. Breaking a preliminary sales agreement more than ten days after the statutory time limit would cost us ten percent of the overall price—a fortune, in other words. It was out of the question. Out of the question for someone of sound mind. Anyone else would have said: "It's just bad luck, rotten luck, not the end of the world." Anyone else would have pouted for an evening and then forgotten about it.

THAT'S WHAT I SHOULD have done. That's what Claude said we should do.

BUT I JUST WOULDN'T give up on my plan, despite the huge effort it was going to entail. I'd take this new can of worms and use it to feed myself. I'd make a deal with the devil.

No, don't do it! That's what the voice should have screamed.

"Just let it go," Claude said. "It has to stop now."

Sleepless nights. Elation. Reflection. Palpitations.

I WANTED THE MERCIERS' house. I wanted to stay in the neighborhood, now that I thought about it, near the cafés, near the school, near the market. How had I let myself get sucked in by a building at the foot of the Montessuy towers, without anything nearby except for the public pool (whose entry fee had become prohibitively expensive, no doubt so that the poor people in the towers wouldn't bother all the social climbers who'd just moved into the neighborhood), and where there weren't any pedestrians because there was no reason to wander about on foot. Had I imagined myself living in this deserted zone just because I'd seen two rabbits frolicking in the grass one morning? Just because I thought Claude could keep his instruments in an unheated wooden shack in a shared courtyard, without even knowing if the homeowners' association would give permission? What was I thinking?

We had to buy the Merciers' house, with its little yard. I felt it, I wanted it—it was the opportunity of a lifetime.

CLAUDE WAS SLEEPING PEACEFULLY, and I didn't dare wake him up to tell him I'd figure something out. My head was spinning as I tried to imagine how I'd break the sales agreement. If only I'd fallen asleep too—if only I'd given up on not giving up. There was still time to stop. All I had to do was sit there and do nothing. Just do nothing.

DON'T MOVE A FINGER.

The simplest instructions I'd ever had in my life.

Stay in your bedroom and keep still. That's what the voice whispering in my ear was telling me to do.

THE NEXT DAY, IN my frenzied state, I decided to consult the law books: I became a specialist in promissory letters, obligations, and everything required to break agreements. I made inquiries with the notary (who was a friend), the real-estate agency, and the bank, which I'd already visited two weeks before. I made new calculations in my notebook. And once I'd exhausted all the possibilities, or rather all the dead ends, I decided that we'd buy the apartment in Montessuy, as planned, and then immediately sell it. It wasn't really a stroke of genius on my part—demand was high, and I knew plenty of people who were looking for exactly that kind of quiet apartment. It was the new creed of our generation, all these young couples with children who dreamed of sharing a yard with a swing set, sharing a garden with rabbits running through it, sharing an evening drink with the neighbors. There was more demand than supply, which meant I'd be able to sell the place in no time at all. The ad would go something like this: "Rare find. Family-centered. Time outside. Room to barbecue. Garden and joie de vivre."

Of course, I had to talk to Claude about it. He tried to dissuade me, like I knew he would. Anyone with any sense would have done the same thing. But I was the one making the decisions. "I'll take care of everything," I said. "You won't have to lift a finger." And after a slight pause: "Don't worry, it'll all go smoothly."

In other words: Just look how clever I am.

In other other words: I'm not going to pass on any opportunity to amaze you.

I ARRANGED ONE MEETING after another and conducted my own visits of the Montessuy apartment, without going through an agency. I lived in fear of the question that kept coming up: "Why are you selling?" I invented such a trashy lie that I don't dare to write it. It was one of those little compromises we all make with ourselves, even if we're never proud of them. I've never talked about it, not even in a shrink's office. "Why are you selling?"

I'd show the apartment and then go pick up our son from school. It seemed normal. And in fact, everything was going just fine—I was treating it all as a game. The rollercoaster ride had begun. I told myself that I enjoyed all these visits, that I could even do it as a profession if I ever needed to. I'd started to write a new novel, but I couldn't focus on it anymore. I called it *Hide and Seek*, and it was a modern-day version of the fairy tale "Hop o' My Thumb." I ended up dropping it. When you write, you have to be obsessed by the story you're telling, and I was obsessed by something else, something all-consuming.

Thankfully, I had an office to go to, as I've already mentioned, which gave me some balance, at least for a few hours every week. This part of my life kept me sane. I'd drive to my office on the Lyon ring road, take part in meetings, make decisions, hold conversations, talk on the phone, read books—it was all concrete and well-defined. It allowed me to tell myself "Everything's fine, you're not going crazy."

BUT IN THE OTHER part of my life I was lying. I sold the apartment I'd bought three weeks earlier to a young couple who'd just gotten an inheritance (maybe they were lying too) and wanted to start a family. I was proud when I was able to tell Claude.

It was fantastic. A huge relief, because I'd finally gotten a crushing burden off my back. I felt light again. So light! I had a desire to dance that wouldn't go away. All I felt was joy, joy, and more joy.

Now I could call Madame Mercier, whom we'd made to wait after begging her.

DON'T CALL.

EVERYTHING WAS GETTING BACK to normal, I thought, after that uncontrolled acceleration. Everything was working out perfectly well.

Selling our silk workshop was relatively easy, even though the sun only came in between one and three p.m. (it was the end of winter), barely giving us time to show off the stone walls and parquet floor we'd sanded with such conviction ten years earlier. After all, the neighborhood was in the middle of a boom. A young couple (yet another one) from Saint-Étienne—the guy was a fireman—found the apartment to their liking, and planned to rip everything out and start from scratch. Maybe they'd even revive the tradition of drop ceilings; the guy didn't like the idea of the beams catching fire. To each his own obsessions.

We still had to sign the sales agreement for the Merciers' house, and get a loan from the bank, which would allow us to get back on our feet. I remember Claude joking around one day, as we sat in the Crédit Mutuel office with our motorcycle helmets on our laps, about how we'd divide the loan insurance between us. In case of death, of course.

Should we go fifty-fifty? Forty-sixty? It was like trying to figure out who had the most value—not just who was more reliable or more solvent, but who had the more promising future. I had a part-time office job at a nonprofit and was just starting out as a writer. Claude was running the music section at the Bibliothèque Municipale de Lyon (the city's public library) and working regularly for *Le Monde* (usually the Rhône-Alpes edition), writing articles about music. We arm-wrestled on the desk at the Crédit Mutuel, right in front of the financial adviser, laughing the whole time, to make up for how serious we'd been while we initialed every page of the contract we hadn't read. It was an instinctive reflex of postadolescent rebellion, and our immature attitude showed that we weren't truly comfortable buying a house—it was our dream, but deep down we disdained it. Somehow it just wasn't us. And yet we went full speed ahead into this new stage of our lives.

I DIDN'T REALIZE IT at the time, but I'd just paved the way for the accident, and I'd done so of my own free will.

4

If only we hadn't asked for the keys in advance

WE'D AGREED THAT THE MERCIERS WOULD GIVE US the keys to the house on Monday, June 21, the date we'd be signing the bill of sale. But we were too impatient for that, and we begged them to hand over the keys a few days early, on Friday, June 18, so we could use the weekend to clear a bit of space in the garage, bring over a few boxes, and thus begin the move. The notary was a friend, as I've mentioned. Or rather, he was Guy's friend—Guy worked with Claude at the library. The notary, seeing how insistent we were, allowed us to slightly bend the rules, because he wanted to be nice to us and not behave like an inflexible officer of the law. He figured he was doing us a favor, and after all it was no big deal—it happened all the time. We just had to take out house insurance right away, which we were only too happy to do. We began to bring over the first few boxes, winter clothes, books, records, a few toys. We thought we were saving time. And since the apartment we were leaving was only a few hundred yards from the house, we could bring things over whenever we felt like it, just by loading up our Peugeot 106.

STUFFING THE CAR WITH bags and boxes was fun, like going back to our student days. We had a great time sorting, making piles, setting everything into motion. We felt an urge to act after all these months of hemming and hawing. We wanted to get into the new place so badly that it was impossible for us to sit still. We were electric, and we undertook even the slightest movement with an impatience that bordered on euphoria. I was just as restless as the day I left home to move in with Claude in the center of Lyon. It's the kind of vigorous feeling that marks you, that leaves its traces on your body. The new house really got our imaginations going, and the only limit was our budget.

I COULD ALREADY SEE myself loosening the soil, organizing, planting. I imagined a little botanical garden where our son could grow carnivorous plants, which were his new passion. I could already see myself building a miniature greenhouse, where I could grow seedlings. I was imagining a sunroom and all sorts of other extensions. There was no problem coming up with ideas. In fact, the opposite was true—every plan led to new plans. It's amazing how the mind occupies space and projects itself, endlessly exploring every square foot of newly acquired land.

I REMEMBER THE WEEKEND when we got the keys as a gift. I remember the June light making patterns on the rammed earth walls; I remember the big wooden door to the property, its ancient frame, the firm grip required to open and close it, the heavy key that was hard to turn in the rusty lock. I remember the bright sunlight reflecting on the white-hot inner courtyard, and I remember my desire to fill this courtyard with climbing plants, to turn it into a patio, a sanctum inspired by the Mediterranean. I liked the idea of entering the house by way of this garden that we'd have to invent. I imagined building a little bike shed in a corner, because in this new and better world, I saw myself taking my bike to do my shopping, like the ultra-cool city dweller I expected to become. Back then, the term *urban liberal* hadn't been invented yet.

WE WENT TO THE Feyssine Flea Market on Sunday morning and found a wrought-iron outdoor table with matching chairs, a little worn down but still in working order. I'd just have to sand and repaint them. This charming and rustic outdoor furniture was a perfect snapshot of our future life as I imagined it—a snapshot I'd no doubt gleaned from movies, or from the home-decorating magazines I spent my time feverishly flipping through, which I kept on a shelf that's still there, right behind me, in the little room where I write, which will soon be razed to the ground like everything else.

We invited Marie and Marc to have a drink with us in our backyard, on the rather uncomfortable wrought-iron chairs. We drank beer that we'd brought over for the occasion—it was like a little picnic. We sat beneath the cherry tree that was weighed down with cherries because it was right in the middle of the season. The cherries fell on the ground, burst on the gravel, got stuck to our shoes. The boys climbed up into the tree. I shouted at them to be careful; after all, it would have been terrible to ruin such a beautiful Sunday.

AND YET HERE WE are.
     We never should have asked for those keys in advance.
     Those couple of days made all the difference.
     I didn't understand until later.

DON'T TAKE THE KEYS.

5

If only I hadn't phoned my mother

FAMILY WORKINGS ARE STRANGE. YOUR OWN BUSI-
ness sometimes ends up being displayed for others to see. Or
rather, to hear. Without you knowing it. My mother knew
that my brother, who also lived in Lyon, needed somewhere to park his motorcycle. Just for a week. Because of
his landlord, who, from what I understood later, would
need the garage to be empty so he could paint it. Starting
on June 18—the very day we'd be getting the keys. Which
was also the day my brother was supposed to leave for his
vacation. I wonder why I told my mother that we had the
keys, that we already had the keys, that we finally had the
keys. What was so urgent about it?

I wonder why I told my mother that there was a garage
attached to the house. A garage we wanted to turn into a
living room. And a yard where we'd figure out a place to
build a garage.

WHAT MAKES A DAUGHTER blurt something out to her mother right as it's happening? We didn't even call each other very often, maybe every two weeks; the fact that cell phones hadn't been invented yet kept us from sending incessant texts to share the slightest changes in our location or state of mind, the way we do today. (I realize cell phones *had* been invented, but we hadn't bought one yet; the only one of my close circle of friends who had one was Clarisse, who was in a relationship with a married man, and would pull her huge GSM phone out of her bag with a knowing look every time she visited us, trying to find a signal.)

IT WOULD ALSO HAVE been possible for me to call my mother and get the answering machine instead. When I say "call my mother," I really mean "call my parents"—this slip of the tongue speaks volumes. But since my father didn't hear well, and no doubt also for other reasons, he'd gotten into the habit of not answering the phone. In any case, I wouldn't have left a message, which would have prevented everything that happened afterward. But my parents rarely went out, especially at night, which meant that in reality, there was no chance of getting the answering machine. No chance. Which is both reassuring and frightening. My mother, by contrast, often had a hard time reaching me, which led her to leave messages asking: "Where are you off gallivanting now?" using a term full of innuendo to suggest that I didn't know how to stay in one place.

I guess I had nothing more interesting to say to my

mother than to tell her I'd gotten the keys in advance. And it was, after all, a bit of good news. "Mom, I got the keys!" said the daughter, all too excited. In the same way she might have said: "Mom, look, I made pee-pee in my potty!" Mom, I got the keys; Mom, I can buy a house, just like a grown-up. I did it all just like you taught me. Just because I listen to the Sex Pistols doesn't mean I can't be like my parents.

HOW OLD DO YOU have to be to stop trying to impress your mother?

DID I WANT HER to see how the notary had rewarded us by treating us like friends? Was I trying to make my mother think more highly of me when I mentioned in passing that the notary was a friend? I wouldn't have used these words at the time, but I'd embarked on what's called a rise in social status, and I wasn't spared from the neurosis that goes along with it, no doubt like many of those around me. As I said in the previous chapter, the notary was a friend of a friend; we hadn't known him for long. And it's only natural, in conversations, to turn friends of friends, and even mere acquaintances, into friends, just to simplify things. That's how it is. People like shortcuts. You can't spend your life getting bogged down in details.

WHAT IS IT THAT makes a mother retain a piece of information and then promptly transmit it to her son? Brigitte has the keys to a house with a garage. David needs a garage. I'll get things moving, I'll be the organizer, I'll put my son in touch with my daughter, I'll make myself useful. Thanks, Mom. It's only natural—it's that enthusiasm that makes family members dependent on each other. I'd have done the same thing. In physics, they call it the law of communicating vessels. It's the very definition of a family. Being a mother means keeping everything balanced, equal—making sure Brigitte doesn't have more mashed potatoes than David. Making sure Brigitte, the eldest daughter, lends her things to David, the younger brother. Lend him your Lego, make sure he's involved, let him use your garage. Everyone's happy. And grateful. It's not meddling, it's just getting people to help each other out. There are no such things as borders or property in a family. You sacrifice yourself for the benefit of the group, or in this case the clan.

AND SO SHE PASSED on the message.

6

If only my brother hadn't suddenly taken a week's holiday

I CAN'T REMEMBER WHERE MY BROTHER WAS WORK-ing in 1999. Maybe he was already working as a service technician for the motor pool at the Rhône department prefecture. What matters is that he had a job that allowed him to take a week's holiday in June, on the spur of the moment, before the real holidays in August. I can't remember if France had already gone to a thirty-five-hour workweek. I could check, but what for? Unless it was his boss who ordered him for administrative reasons to use up the days off or the overtime he'd stored up, because the administration had no intention of paying him for it.

One of his buddies loaned him a studio apartment in Nice, a vacation rental. Maybe he'd had a cancellation—I never did find out. You don't turn down an apartment on the Côte d'Azur, especially when you've spent eleven months breathing exhaust fumes and repairing emergency lights at the Lyon municipality. The light of the Baie des Anges is just a little nicer than the one you find in the stalls where they do the oil changes for the French police's fleet of Renault Masters. My brother had taken care of everything—his superiors, his colleagues, his wife, his daughter's preschool; the only problem left was finding a garage, and I was going to solve this problem in spite of myself. He was leaving on Saturday, June 19, in the morning, and we'd just gotten the keys. Chance had taken care of everything. Just wheel your Honda CBR900 Fireblade over here, put it in the corner, no one will steal it.

7

If only I'd allowed our son to go on vacation with my brother

BUT MY BROTHER, WITHOUT EVEN REALIZING IT, had given us a way out. A wild card that we should have played.

Since he was conscientious and generous, he offered to bring our son along for an unexpected week in the sun. I remember our telephone conversation. All I had to do was say yes for the accident not to happen. All I had to do was jump for joy at the idea that our son could skip the final week of his first year of primary school, that he could miss the end-of-year party and the festivities of those last few days. But instead I said we'd think about it, I'd talk to Claude, we'd call him back soon.

Don't think. Say yes.

THE LITTLE VOICE IN my head would have just had to whisper that it was important for our son to spend a week with his cousin and his uncle, far more important than school, that it was the perfect occasion to strengthen those family ties everyone talks about. I'd have just needed to be normal. But in fact I was terrified. Here's the question I'd have asked if I'd conducted a survey of my friends: Who would allow her eight-year-old son, who can barely swim, to spend an entire week at the seaside with two adults she doesn't see very often, and thus has no idea how closely they'd watch the kids; two adults, furthermore, who (as she heard from her mother) would have access to a motorboat that's moored nearby; and all this in a studio apartment separated from the beach by a busy road?

CLAUDE AND I FELT ridiculous as we went back and forth, and we were embarrassed when we declined the invitation. Who did we think we were to refuse an offer like this? Why were we being so suspicious? Were we killjoys, or just so scared that we couldn't trust anyone? We knew we'd be busy working on the house, but we'd already registered our son in a summer camp for two weeks in August, and those two weeks away from him seemed like enough.

I called my brother back and told him a little white lie. I said his nephew had end-of-year tests, and that it wouldn't be appropriate for him to miss them. This wasn't true. I said he had an important role in the dance routine his class had been preparing for the end-of-year party, which, fortunately for my conscience, was true. I could sense his disappointment and his doubts about my honesty. "Well, that's a shame. Sophie's gonna be so disappointed." Sophie worshipped her cousin—he'd taught her how to climb over the fence at their grandparents' place, how to sneak out and spend the night in the garden shed, and how to feed the horses without getting her hands bitten.

It really was a shame. But I felt liberated because I hadn't endangered our son. We'd been able to say no without offending anyone.

Once again, it was the wrong decision.

8

If only my brother hadn't had a garage issue

I NEVER UNDERSTOOD MY BROTHER'S ARRANGE-
ment for the garage he rented in his neighborhood. I guess
it was more of a sublet. He shared a space in a communal
garage with a friend of his, this woman from his gym, or
maybe she was a colleague from the police department.
There's always room for one more motorcycle, she'd told
him, even one with a huge engine. It was a good tip—the
place was close to where he lived. My brother always gets
good tips, whether it's for a dishwasher, a burglar alarm,
or shock absorbers for a delivery van.

It was the perfect arrangement, you might say, except
that he had to find somewhere else to park his motorcycle
from Friday, June 18, until Saturday, the twenty-fifth.
This minor problem soon turned into a complete headache.
He asked his friends, his colleagues, the other parents at
his daughter's school, and even the supervisor at the police

motor pool, in other words his boss. But there weren't any good options, and soon he'd have to ask his Honda to sleep under the stars. This was the worst thing imaginable for my brother, who was (and still is) a die-hard biker, much more serious than Claude—and even Claude wouldn't have let his Suzuki LS650 Savage spend the night outside.

My brother was already thinking he'd have to bribe the cop who supervised the main garage of the Ministry of the Interior, which surely wouldn't be affected by a single motorcycle stashed in a corner. But it's always the same story: you make one exception, and pretty soon it's anarchy. And if it's anarchy, it's not the police anymore.

Maybe he'd have tried his friend from the go-kart club again, or chased up his brother-in-law; maybe he'd have slipped a couple hundred francs to the caretaker of his building to get access to the cellar; maybe he'd have slipped a case of wine to a friend of a friend; maybe in the end he'd have found some solution that would allow him to take his holiday. But then my mother called with her precious bit of news: Brigitte's getting the keys. Brigitte's getting the keys in advance. Brigitte's getting the keys on Friday the eighteenth in the afternoon, the notary made a little exception, if you see what I mean, just make sure it stays between us. Isn't this an amazing coincidence? Sometimes life gives you these little gifts.

9

If only I hadn't changed the date of my trip to see my publisher in Paris

MY SECOND NOVEL WAS DUE TO BE PUBLISHED IN September, or, to be more precise, at the very end of August. It was called *Nico*. My press attaché said I should come up to Paris to promote the book, which at this stage mainly meant writing dedications in the copies that would be sent to journalists, who would read it in the summer. At first she suggested Friday, June 18, but that was the day I'd be getting the keys, and I didn't want to put off everything I've just talked about. We also had an appointment with a heating specialist, which I didn't want to miss. I asked if I could wait until the following week—say, Tuesday, June 22—to come to Paris. Which was annoying, because upending your press attaché's schedule like that isn't something you're supposed to do. But Emmanuelle was lovely, charming, accommodating, even though she should have told me where to go. She should have said: I'm the one who makes these decisions.

It's June eighteenth or never, my dear. It's not up to you.

TO TOP IT OFF, I'd already gotten my train ticket, which unfortunately I could exchange, as long as I was willing to go stand in line at the SNCF offices in the Croix-Rousse neighborhood. Today I curse that exchangeable ticket. They should have made me keep the old one. I curse this world that bent itself to my wishes. I curse this freedom that I made such poor use of.

If I'd gone to Paris on June 18, as planned, I'd have returned in the evening, at the very moment my brother was dropping off his motorcycle. We'd have crossed paths for a few seconds. And that's it. Nothing else would have happened.

I HAD TO WAIT for a good twenty minutes at the SNCF offices, number in hand, but since I was in an excellent mood, it was no big deal, even when I was sitting face-to-face with an agent whose slow movements and deep detachment seemed like nothing less than a riddle. This was before the self-serve terminals—before the all-encompassing digital realm made us all our own ticket agents, typists, secretaries, and accountants. I was elated, I think, by the idea of a trip to Paris and staying at Hélène's place. Elated by the idea that I'd soon have my novel in my hands. Everything was perfect.

PARISIANS DON'T REALIZE IT, but for us provincials, the simple fact of getting a train ticket and having a place to sleep in Paris is a minor accomplishment. To stay with friends, you first need to have friends in the capital—all the better if they actually live in the city rather than the suburbs, and don't have too many kids. Since I'd only published one book, I just knew a few people from the publishing world, and not well enough to expect any of them to offer me a place to stay. And in any case, I'd always hated sleeping on a couch in the living room, which meant having to show my morning face (which is very different from my evening face), imposing on others to use the shower, and invading the privacy of these friends, my friends from Paris, who are sadly invisible to me most of the time, and whom my friends from Lyon will never meet. (Well, except for the day of my funeral.)

My publisher, Stock, offered to book me a hotel room, which was only natural, since I had to be at their office around ten a.m.—I'd have to get up at the crack of dawn if I were coming from Lyon. I'd already made them change the date, so I didn't want to ask them to change the time as well. I decided to be accommodating and decline the hotel room, which, as I knew, would be an added expense, especially as they were already paying for my train ticket. I've never liked the way publishers see writers from outside Paris as purveyors of expense claims—it's already complicated enough being called a "regional writer." Things have changed a little, but back then, being a writer meant living in Paris, which meant you could just drop by your publisher's office on the way to the grocery store. I was always the one who arrived by train, the one who was defined by a timetable. When people didn't know what to say to me, they asked me if I had a train to catch, just to have something to talk about. I could never go along for impromptu happy hours, because the last train from the Gare de Lyon left at 7:58 p.m. I can't count the number of times I've sprinted for that train.

SINCE I WASN'T VERY experienced, I took the book promo seriously—I'm a serious girl, after all. I wanted to leave the night before, since this would keep me from having to get up at five in the morning (after not having slept), and would allow me to see Hélène, a friend from Lyon who'd just started working in a bookstore in the twentieth arrondissement, and who insisted that I visit her. Strangely, it was perfect timing.

OF COURSE, YOU HAVE to see an art exhibit when you go to Paris. Those of us who live in the provinces see exhibits as aims in themselves, because we think that where we live, we're deprived of something essential—namely, Klimt, Bacon, or Boltanski—and we imagine Parisians spending their lives strolling past Walker Evans photos or installations at the Fondation Cartier. For us, Paris is synonymous with exhibits and mythical concerts. It's all part and parcel of "the provincial complex": the province dweller, after all, is the one who hasn't seen the exhibit, who settles for saying she's heard about it, who's constrained to leafing through the arts supplements of newspapers.

The province dweller has of course heard all about the Joy Division concert at the Bains Douches in 1979, but she never actually saw the group—she had to content herself with reading Michka Assayas's magnificent review in *Libération*. All of this made Claude green with envy, and fanned his desire to write about rock. Exhibits, concerts, and mythical venues like the Bataclan, the Maroquinerie, the Élysée Montmartre, the Gibus, the Trabendo, or the Olympia, not to mention the Palace, were all in Paris, which was the place where everything happened—at least that's how it seemed.

SO I TOLD MYSELF that I'd sleep at Hélène's on June 21, write my dedications the next day, and if I had time afterward I'd go see Ousmane Sow's installation on the Pont des Arts. I'd aim to take the 6:58 train on that Tuesday, June 22, which would get me back to Lyon around nine.

IT COULDN'T HAVE WORKED out any better.
Or so I thought.

10

If only I'd phoned Claude on the evening of June 21 as I should have, instead of listening to Hélène tell me about her latest romance

I SAID GOODBYE TO CLAUDE ON MONDAY, JUNE 21, in the early afternoon, after we signed for the sale at the notary's office.

I took the bus to the train station, and then I took the train, exactly as planned. I spent the evening at Hélène's place, exactly as planned. Over the weekend we'd tinkered on the house, but I'd also run into a friend at the supermarket. Her son was in the same class as ours, and she invited us to his eighth birthday party on the afternoon of Tuesday, June 22. After-school invitations like this one were common, and this camaraderie that just went without saying, the favors we all did for each other, was another reason I wanted to stay in the same neighborhood. Everything was easy.

THIS MEANT CLAUDE WOULDN'T have to pick up his son at school.

I'd completely forgotten to tell him.

Another wild card.

I'D FORGOTTEN.

But I'd sort it out.

I'd interrupt the conversation I was having with Hélène, who lived close to the Centre Pompidou, and whom I hadn't seen for a long time. I'd get up from the couch, where I was comfortably settled and where I'd be sleeping that night, I'd ask to use the phone, I'd wait until nine thirty, because back then, as I'm sure you'll remember, back then long-distance calls were expensive, there were different rates depending on the distance, there were schedules, a whole protocol that sometimes made life stupid, like when you had to wait near the phone if you were expecting a call, especially an official call, or one from someone you were in love with.

We'd gotten into a conversation, but I can't remember exactly what we were talking about. Hélène was probably telling me about her new job in the bookstore, or about the woman she'd just met, who made her heart race and caused her sleepless nights. Or maybe we'd been discussing the books of Olivier Cadiot, whom she loved, or Cat Power's latest album, which she'd just put on the turntable. Yes, we were likely listening to *Moon Pix*. Maybe we were talking about the house we'd just bought, Claude and I, and all the work we'd have to do on it, since we planned to have three bedrooms upstairs, one of which would be a guest room that she could use whenever she wanted.

Get up and call him.

THERE'S STILL TIME TO prevent what's about to happen.

WE WERE EATING PASTRIES she'd heated up (they were delicious) and having a drink, taking little sips of Martini Rosso. We drank and we chatted. It had just gone nine thirty, and the World Music Day concert was reaching a crescendo on the street below her apartment. I could see a clock in the corner of the kitchenette, so I was able to keep track of time. I told myself that it was still early, that Claude would be putting his son to bed. I didn't want to bother him right then, because he'd probably want to be alone for a while, smoking a Lucky Strike at the window and listening to one of the new CDs he'd brought home from the office with the bass turned up. He could listen on high volume until ten; after that, the neighbors had the right to complain, though they never had—in fact, they were the ones filling our ears with Erik Satie's *Gymnopédies*, played on a piano with no dampers, not to mention their frequent spats that always ended the same way, with the girl's sobs filtering through the ceiling that had no insulating layer, since, as I mentioned earlier, we'd removed the lattice.

SOMETHING KEPT ME FROM calling. I was putting it off. I looked over at the telephone receiver, which was sitting on one of the lower shelves of the bookcase, but I just couldn't interrupt Hélène, who was telling me intimate details about herself, her new life in Paris, her romantic adventures. I didn't dare get up and ask her if I could use her phone to call Claude; I was afraid she'd find it tacky, not to mention annoying, for a girl who's barely been away from her partner for a few hours to call him. I was probably afraid she'd judge me the way people sometimes judge heterosexual couples—these days they're said to be "heteronormative"—and think I wasn't capable of freedom, of being alone, away from Claude (whom she both knew and liked). And to top it off, I had a nagging worry that she would think I felt obliged to call because I had a child, which would lead her to think, or indeed to confirm, that mothers are nothing without their kids.

Because the clichés aren't just about heteronormative couples. There are also plenty of clichés about mothers who find life hard when they're away from their children, who aren't able to talk about or think about anything but their kids. And it has to be said that there's some truth to this. I recently read, in a book called *La folie maternelle ordinaire* ("everyday maternal madness"), an essay by the Lacanian psychoanalyst Dominique Guyomard, who asks the thorny question of whether you can be a mother without being crazy. And the question basically contains the answer. Hélène didn't have a man or a child in her life, and I didn't want to pollute her with what may have been my own maternal madness—a madness that, in retrospect, partially explains my actions.

But if I'm being honest, I just didn't want to interrupt what she was telling me about her love life, which was giving me a kind of thrill that evening. It was like we were regressing to the time when we were schoolgirls, indulging each other, egging each other on. And it was also simple laziness—I couldn't be bothered to get up. I just didn't feel like it.

I SAID TO MYSELF: It doesn't matter what you're feeling. Go call him right this minute.

It was then that I should have called.

I could never have guessed it, but that phone call would have changed the course of our lives.

11

If only I'd had a cell phone

All well? No need to pick Théo up from school tomorrow, he's been invited to Maxime's birthday party, he'll get a ride with Maxime's mom, she'll drive him home afterwards. Here's her number. Good night, my love.

It was just past ten, which would have been the perfect moment to burst into Claude's evening. He'd have turned the music down, and maybe he'd be drinking a beer while writing an article. But I still didn't dare interrupt what Hélène was confiding in me, these words that were very private and that flattered me with the trust they showed. I couldn't, not right in the middle of a sentence, not right in the middle of a story (she was a master at building up suspense), not when she was trying to figure out her feelings for this woman she'd just met. Getting up at that point would have been like telling her I had something better to do than listen to her. Sorry, this is really interesting but my mind is elsewhere, excuse me a moment, I just have to call Claude, there's something we need to sort out.

I didn't dare, because calls between Paris and Lyon were expensive, and phoning, even after nine thirty, would have meant asking another favor of this friend who was already putting me up, even if I know that this phony excuse is no excuse at all.

Let's just say that you have to take it all into account, this bundle of microreasons that, when you put them together, begin to form an impediment to calling.

JUST AS THE MICROEVENTS that had taken place that week ended up weaving a web strong enough to lead inexorably to the accident.

But there's another reason. The real one.

And it may be that this real reason alone is what kept me from phoning.

How can I deal with it in a way that makes me seem credible—credible, first and foremost, to myself?

WHAT KEPT ME FROM getting up from the couch between nine thirty and ten thirty was a strange feeling that had been growing in me for several years, brought on by the time in which we were living: a feeling that fathers had to forge a new place in the home. I wanted Claude not to need me, not to need my viewpoints and opinions to take care of his son. I wanted (but this is the wrong verb), I was hoping that he would affirm his presence, and that he would build a relationship with his son, which he was doing. People often say of mothers that they're overbearing and all-consuming—and indeed mad, as I just mentioned—so I tried to lurk in the background from time to time, never knowing if I was doing too much or not enough. I tried to give them room.

Serious newspapers were full of articles that looked at dads in a new way, asking them to become what people back then called "new fathers"—in other words, less virile, less distant, and less scarce. Less wedged between their jobs and their evenings in front of the television, like the clichéd average French man of previous generations, those silent father figures who smoked Gauloises in the car, who put their feet on the table, who told their wives to do the ironing. And who had only a moderate interest in their progeny.

The nineties asked these new fathers to go beyond protecting the home and providing for their families. They'd now be required to do other things as well, such as participating in natural childbirth courses, or learning to feed babies and change their diapers. This affected the balance of many couples, because women started to get impatient when their husbands couldn't put on a onesie properly. This new role for the father had to be invented. Women had to learn to share, which meant simultaneously hoping for the best and fearing the worst. They had to deal with opposing desires, demands dictated by their mothers but also by an evolving society and by their own convictions, not to say their own neuroses. Which meant pleasing a lot of people.

THIS IS NO DOUBT what kept me from acting that evening at Hélène's place. I remember the words I kept hearing in my head: Leave the boys alone, let them manage on their own. It sprang from my feminist attitude and my desire to affirm my independence. Deep down, I didn't want to call—I didn't want to know what they'd eaten, how they'd spent the evening, if our son had done his homework, what time he'd gone to bed, what Claude was going to wear the next day. Of course I did want to know, I was burning with the desire to know, but a little voice told me to leave them alone.

Leave them be. You're not indispensable.

I WATCHED THE MINUTES tick by and told myself that Claude would be writing his article on PJ Harvey, who was opening her tour at the Transbordeur in Villeurbanne. I imagined him smoking, window open onto the June night, taking a break between two paragraphs. No doubt he'd hear the distant harmonies of the World Music Day concert as they filtered through the streets. I could see him putting PJ Harvey's latest record, *Is This Desire?*, onto the turntable, listening attentively to that voice and those guitar chords, preparing questions for the interview he was hoping to do. The newspaper had asked him to write a profile, a perilous endeavor that consists in blending biographical and musical data and choosing an interesting angle—you had to find the angle, this was the watchword of every journalist, the word that had kept him in its clutches from the moment he began working as a freelancer for *Le Monde* five or six years earlier.

I STILL WANTED TO call because I wasn't completely at peace. But because of all my hesitating, it was almost eleven o'clock, and it would be ridiculous to call so late for such an unimportant message. Claude was already planning to pick up his son, which was something that gave him a lot of pleasure. And that's what I ended up realizing: going to the school to get his son was a joy for him, not a chore. How had I not thought of this earlier? He'd see his son before the birthday party; maybe they'd even go there together. They'd have plenty of things to talk about, things I wouldn't have understood. They'd joke around on the drive over, they'd have fun. I decided it was none of my business. It was their life. Claude was an adult, and that was that.

12

If only mommy time hadn't also been daddy time

WHAT MAKES A FATHER WHO HAS RESPONSIBILITIES, who manages a department in an important establishment (Lyon's municipal library), pick up his son from school twice a week, and even make it a priority? It was unusual for men at the end of the twentieth century, especially those who worked in management, to interrupt their workday at 4:00 p.m.—to decide their presence was no longer necessary and leave to go spend time with their kids. It wasn't something most women would do either, even though they go to amazing lengths to reconcile their family lives, their professional lives, and their relationships. But so much has already been said about this subject. We all do what we can with the time we have, the moments we can scrape together. As parents, we're constantly frustrated by missing important things. Constantly counting our seconds from morning to night, so we can revel in the

"Whew" we utter when we can finally turn off the light in the kids' room.

I once knew an editor—in fact he was my editor at the time, Jean-Marc Roberts (it's a real pleasure to mention him)—who used to leave his office every day at five to pick his son up from school. He no doubt had better things to do at that hour. After all, he worked right in the middle of Paris, where high-stakes games are being played at every table. I don't know how he managed, but he showed up at the school every day, at the time we refer to in French as *l'heure des mamans*, mommy time.

CLAUDE WAS ONE OF those men who organize their lives like this. He was there every Tuesday and every Thursday, no matter what happened, and he never lost his composure, his elegance, and even, I daresay, his virility. He experienced, in the simplest way, the pleasure of a father picking up his son, and this activity truly made him blossom. It sounds old-fashioned to put it like that, but after all, having kids ages you.

HE ALSO WASN'T ONE of those men who are always saying that they're snowed under, that they have too much going on, as so many people do today. Despite the fact that he had two jobs—at the library and the newspaper—he never lost his cool, never became less available, even though turning in his articles on time and managing a team of fifteen people could really raise his stress level. I never saw him brag, or treat those beneath him with anything but respect; I never saw him try to crush anyone, least of all me. I, on the other hand, was so disorganized that I sometimes broke down in tears. When I think about it now, I can see that he prioritized the things that pleased him, and picking up his son from school no doubt gave him more pleasure than setting up endless meetings with other bosses—it brought him the balance that kept him standing, and that made him so dreamy, so seductive.

I CAN'T REMEMBER IF my father ever came to get me and my brother at school. If I hadn't written these lines, I'd never have asked myself the question. No, my mother had stopped working to raise us, which was normal in the seventies, and she was the one who organized shifts with the other women to come get us until the end of primary school, to guide us across the two main roads that separated our apartment from the schools, several blocks away. All the women in the neighborhood took part. None of the men. Even though my father did shift work at the post office, and had every second afternoon off. It's a mystery.

WHAT'S CERTAIN IS THAT the school, school hours, the end of the school day, school vacations, this whole hourly, daily, and seasonal rhythm is the basis of how parents organize their lives, and we were no exception.

If the accident hadn't happened, I might not have remembered the arrangement Claude and I made to divvy up the days of the week. I would never have thought back on how I drove like a maniac along the ring road every

Monday and Friday, coming back from the suburb where I worked, and how I was often the last parent to arrive in front of the school gate, my heart pounding and my stomach in knots, having gone way over the speed limit, accelerated through yellow lights, and driven way too close to the cars in front of me, as if the fact that I was in a hurry would make them go faster.

If the accident hadn't happened, I would never have questioned that obsession we have, those of us who work, with leaving the office at the last minute, which stresses us out and makes us leave everything to chance and hope for miracles. I remember the radio station I used to listen to in the car and the horror I would feel whenever they gave the time. I'd barely reached the off-ramp of the ring road, and the teacher was already letting class out; I was stuck behind a delivery van, and the students had already put on their jackets; I was crawling along in traffic, and they'd already crossed the schoolyard; I was sitting in a line of cars at the traffic light, and my son was probably waiting for me at the front entrance. I remember that it always worked out—barely, but it always worked out. Whew.

13

If only my brother hadn't parked his motorcycle in the garage at the new house

IT'S LIKE A CHILD'S GAME. OR A SENTENCE YOU LEARN to construct at primary school: My brother parks his motorcycle in the garage. Subject, verb, direct object, indirect object.

I've always been obsessed by the way we occupy space. Who does what in our private spaces, our houses and apartments; who sleeps in which room, who takes naps on the living room couch, who monopolizes the bathroom? How do we move about in the hallways and on the stairs; how do we avoid each other, bother each other, spy on each other? How do we organize our lives in those extensions we call balconies, patios, garden sheds, garages?

IT WAS THE FIRST time we ever had our own garage. And we knew what a privilege it was. Until then, Claude had been renting a stall for his Suzuki in a shared garage three blocks from our apartment, just in front of the primary school. Those who live with bikers know all about the attention (an attention that borders on obsession) they pay to garages and all the questions that surround them—how much they cost, how far away they are, whether they have waiting lists. Claude had had several motorbikes stolen, which made his garage all the more important. The garage is also the place where the biker works on his bike, where he keeps his wrenches, motor oil, lubricants, and the shammies he uses to shine the chrome. Our conversations were riddled with references to that indispensable place; one of his most common phrases was: "I'm off to do some work at the garage." It was a necessary extension of our apartment, an exclusive domain that I wanted nothing to do with—it was too bare, too gritty, too humid, and all in all too hostile. I wasn't familiar with its codes: I didn't know how to move around without getting dirty, without walking on an oil stain or knocking over a gas can. And it stunk.

CLAUDE OFTEN WENT TO work at the garage after school let out, and our son became a pro at changing headlight bulbs and tightening brake cables (this was before the arrival of disc brakes). The garage was the place where father and son spoke a wordless language made up of gestures and patience—the patience required to fiddle with an electric lamp so they could see the part of the bike they wanted to tinker with. It was their private kingdom, their little hiding place, the site of that part of their lives that didn't include me.

Garages were always cold. I remember Claude and I sought refuge in one when we were eighteen to escape from prying eyes in our suburb. He already had a motorcycle at the time, and I think that's what I found attractive about him. I would always see him holding his helmet with that huge pair of leather gloves that he never knew what to do with once he'd gotten off the bike.

When Claude and his son came home from the garage, they usually had frozen hands and red cheeks. And grease on the knees of their pants. And that sparkle in their eyes that I loved.

I'M PUTTING OFF THE moment when I'll have to talk about my brother's motorcycle. The one he parked in the garage at the new house. The motorcycle I'll have to deal with at some length. Because it wasn't just any old motorcycle.

14

Why Tadao Baba, the Japanese engineer who revolutionized Honda's history, has forced his way into my life

HOW COULD I EVER HAVE IMAGINED THAT JAPAN, A country I've never set foot in, located almost six thousand miles from my nerve center, would determine the course of my life, or rather destroy it, by way of one of the most prestigious motorcycle manufacturers in the world, and the engineer, Tadao Baba, who designed the famous Honda CBR900 Fireblade, which Claude was riding on the day of the accident?

Japan is a country that many of my friends in France venerate. Some of them even try to live Japanese-style, eating at tables low to the ground, using chopsticks instead of forks, espousing the precepts of Shintoism, and getting involved with Japanese women, who, I admit, possess a unique blend of elegance, refinement, and seductiveness.

It's a country whose literature I'm somewhat familiar with and whose recent history I know quite well. The French writer Philippe Forest, in his novel *Sarinagara* (which means "and yet"), views the Japanese as combining private mourning with the collective mourning of a nation that lost a great many people to the atomic bomb.

It's a country that at once demands respect and inspires fear, both with its code of honor (which the entire world could learn from) and its staggering technological feats, to which both musicians and bikers attest, as they venerate the brands—Honda, Yamaha, Kawasaki, Suzuki, Sony, Casio, and Hitachi—whose products have given them sound, speed, precision, and thrills. Everyone knows the Yamaha DX7 revolutionized pop music in the eighties, featuring prominently, for example, on Prince's album *Around the World in a Day*. Claude was obviously no exception to this rule when he bought his first keyboard: Sequential Circuits, which I mentioned in the first pages of this book, was an American company that had been acquired by Yamaha.

I'd have liked to meet Tadao Baba, the Japanese engineer behind this impressive motorcycle. I wanted to see what he looked like, so I went online and found a portrait of him, smiling, full of charm, cigarette in hand and slightly yellowed teeth. He's in his sixties, and he looks sensational. I even found T-shirts with his photo (taken by Roland Brown): handsome face, salt-and-pepper mane, and underneath, in capital letters: BABA. Fifty-fifty cotton-polyester blend. Only €14.91 on a website called Pixels

Shopping. As I looked around the site, I found the same photo of Tadao Baba printed on an array of products: coffee mugs, bath towels, tote bags, spiral notebooks, shower curtains, duvet covers, yoga mats, iPhone cases, greeting cards. I concluded from all this that Tadao Baba is a star. And I sat there flabbergasted. A shower curtain with his face on it? Good lord.

HONDA ASKED TADAO BABA to design the CBR900 Fireblade as a professional racing bike. The idea was to imagine an inline four-cylinder that could take over from the legendary Honda RVF750 endurance bike to compete in the Suzuka 8 Hours, the famous race outside of Kyoto. I had to check the meaning of "inline four-cylinder engine," though I suspected it had to do with cylinders arranged in a line (I mean, duh), which I can now confirm. While I was checking, the term *carburetor* came into my mind, from the title of the book Claude was reading, and I confirmed that the Honda CBR900 was indeed equipped with a carburetor, and not electronic fuel injection, which practically all vehicles have today.

Sorry for going into such detail, but according to a website dedicated to the Fireblade, Tadao Baba was asked to "design a motorcycle with unprecedented braking and handling qualities, a machine as intuitively responsive as a racing bike, but manufactured on a grand scale." I'm quoting this history of the bike, which I've confirmed with the highest levels of Honda's media relations unit, so that you can see the subtlety and the elegance of the language. What it means, in layman's terms, is that they manufactured a professional racing bike disguised as a production bike. It's what you call a trick—pure sleight of hand. Or, in business jargon, marketing genius, which you need in order to maintain your standing in the face of global competition.

THEY SAY TADAO BABA was different from other engineers. He started at Honda at the age of eighteen in 1962 (the company was ten years old at the time), without any formal training—he learned on the job, which is undoubtedly the best teacher. He began by building cylinder heads and crankshafts for small bikes like the CB72 and the CB77, and little by little, he started innovating. They say he was an impulsive man who would test-drive his own models, and that when he started testing the CBR900 he'd fall sometimes—the bike must have thrown him to the ground the same way horses throw riders to the ground in a rodeo. I can't deny that he built his own legend, but I find the whole thing hard to take. Because Tadao did his test rides on enclosed tracks, on courses reserved for that purpose, and not, as was the case for Claude on Tuesday, June 22, 1999, on a busy boulevard in the middle of Lyon.

TADAO BABA WAS ALSO a poet. Of an inspired and subtle sort. Ethereal, elliptical, in the Japanese style. Inside the front fairing of the CBR900 (this was a special feature of the famous 1998 model that Claude was riding), on the left side, he had these words engraved: "For the people who want to know the meaning of light weight."

Light—in every possible sense of the word.

Like secretly having your initials engraved on the inside of a wedding ring.

15

Why was the Honda CBR900 Fireblade, crown jewel of the Japanese motorcycle industry, which Claude was riding on June 22, 1999, reserved for export to Europe and banned in Japan?

BUT IN FACT, SINCE I'VE LOOKED AT EVERYTHING closely, since I was forced to look for what's invisible to the naked eye, I inevitably discovered a few things, including some that were tough to take. If you look hard enough, you're always going to find things you don't like. And as it happens, the thing I liked least was the agreement between Japan and the EU that allowed France and a few other countries to sell the Honda CBR900 Fireblade right from the start, in 1991, when it was one of the highlights of the Paris Motorcycle Fair, even though it was still banned in Japan (or rather, reserved for competition) because it was considered too dangerous. There's a four-minute film from the fair that introduces this new "Super Sport" model, whose performance was comparable to the 1000cc bikes in this category. Subsequent modifications considerably increased its power-to-weight ratio (130 horsepower/400 pounds, for the connoisseurs), allowing it to reach a maximum speed of 170 miles an hour for the model that concerns us here, namely the 1998, or fourth-generation, version. Tadao Baba had been encouraged by his firm to stop at nothing in his quest for performance.

I KEEP COMING BACK to the fact that the bike wasn't put on the market in Japan because it was deemed too dangerous. It's the detail that keeps tripping me up.

I found out about this the week after the accident, on the day of Claude's funeral, when I spoke with his brother-in-law, Paul, a seasoned biker and a fount of knowledge about motorcycle licensing, who spent his childhood with Claude in the Rillieux housing development before marrying Claude's sister Nicole. Not only did he show me a great deal of affection, he also told me something I wasn't expecting, and which has since been confirmed by several friends who ride motorbikes—it seems that it's well known among bikers. They've all heard lots of stories about accidents on the CBR900, which is why they call it an unrideable bike, a bike made for closed circuits, for racetracks.

Paul explained to me that certain models were vetoed by the Japanese authorities, such as the Kawasaki ZXR750 Ninja, which hot-blooded young men from France, Italy, and Spain were falling over themselves to buy, mischievously referring to it as the motorcycle of death or the coffin on wheels. It was the same for the Honda CBR900: a machine for the initiated, a bomb for kamikazes. Both of these bikes were banned by the Japanese, who had no intention of sending their own citizens over a cliff—after all, their roads are often narrow and winding. Their industry distinguished between bikes made for the domestic market and those reserved for export. Every industry does this to some degree, but this one had strange criteria. Paul also told me that French bikers made fun of the Japanese: "We have better bikes than they do, and they're the ones who make them!" As if it were a privilege; as if this freedom were yet another sign that the French were superior to everyone else. They're the ones who manufacture them, but we're the ones who die on them. A little like the weapons that the French arms industry sends overseas. Except that weapons are obviously made for killing.

SOME OF MY FRIENDS told me I should sue. But this wouldn't have changed anything, and I could already see myself spending the rest of my life trying to prove that a man died because of an overly powerful motorcycle. I would have been just like those people who have inhaled asbestos, ingested glyphosate, or been exposed to radiation during military service in the Algerian Sahara. I would have had to gather proof and more proof, and commission experts—it would literally have taken up all my time. And how was I supposed to show that something approved by the French government was actually dangerous? What does "approved" mean, anyways? Who decides that a motorcycle designed for competition is approved for the roads of France, Spain, or Italy? What I found out is that danger, in other words the bike's weight-to-power ratio, isn't among the criteria. The French authorities, the ones responsible for the tests, consider only the following: blinkers, brake lights, rearview mirrors, license plate, emission standards, and decibels. Nothing about danger, though it's true that things are a lot safer these days, with anti-skid devices, wheelie control, ABS brake systems, rain mode . . . all of which must make some difference.

But the bike was approved, which means that Claude should have been able to control it. Which is the whole problem—we'll come back to it later. Because according to the police report, nothing happened that should have caused an accident. Even if it seems obscene that what's considered dangerous for the Japanese isn't for the French. How can this possibly make sense—by virtue of what export treaty, what trade balance, what rules of exchange, what aspect of globalization, what economic criteria?

I spent my time searching, hunting down every trace that would tell me something about this scandal, this anomaly. I'm referring to the traces that have been left on the internet, which barely existed at the time, so there's not much to go on, just a few testimonies, blogs, discussion forums, and online magazines. I wanted to know for sure: Was it Claude or the motorcycle? Was it a matter of destiny, as I suggested before? Was it immaturity, and if so, was it the immaturity of the one who borrowed the bike or the one who lent it to him? Was it an oil slick, a wasp's sting, the sun in his eyes, a cat crossing the road? Was it joy, some kind of enthusiasm that made him accelerate too quickly? Was it the anxiety of the move? It's always important to blame something or someone. Even if that someone is you.

I WENT BACK TO the site of the accident and tried to take everything into account, the fact that he was going from east to west, the pollen from the plane trees at that time of year, the two pedestrian crossings, the bus stop, the location of the trash cans, the parking spaces, the intersection with the rue Jacquier, the gates of the fancy homes all along the boulevard, the names on the mailboxes. All this to look for a sign.

AND THEN, IN 2004, Honda took the deceptive bike off the market. Today their website, a marvel of elegant design, says they discontinued it to make way for the CBR1000 Fireblade, now classed in the "Sport" rather than the "Touring" category, which ended the debate. The title chosen for this section of the site is "Absolute Power." No more ambiguity, and no more troubled past either.

I STILL NEED TO mention the sites of the French motorcycle magazines, such as *Auto Moto*, *Moto Journal*, or *Moto Mag*, where journalists publish essays and commentaries. What I've read there speaks volumes. For example, one writer says that the Honda CBR900 "lets you get up to a nice little speed of 160 mph—though admittedly, you'll be risking your life, and riding at that speed won't exactly be comfortable." Articles like this one have given me an initiation in the language of catastrophe, the poetry of endangerment that electrifies potential thrill seekers.

Another journalist doubles down: "The Honda CBR600 was aggressive, but it didn't have quite enough horsepower to make it truly dangerous. Not so for the CBR900."

And just to bring home the point, we find this interesting observation: "The straight-four engine from the '91 CBR900 has been reworked to increase power and aggressiveness. With the punch it packs, we found it difficult to keep the bike from doing wheelies. Beginners should give it a miss and choose a more suitable model so they don't scare themselves silly—or worse."

Sic.

THIS IS WHAT HAPPENED to Claude when he accelerated at a green light. The bike popped a wheelie, which led him to lose control, which led to the worst thing imaginable. The very thing the magazine articles somberly predicted.

"TO DO A WHEELIE" means that the bike's front wheel comes off the ground. Other than bikers, no one used the term back then. These days it's all the rage, what with the recent "rodeos" on the outskirts of cities, which are nothing more than high-speed wheelie contests.

I'd never have believed that my life would at times be reduced to gleaning information from motorcycle websites. I wasn't trying to play the victim. I just wanted to find a little community, to locate others who had also had to deal with the harm this bike has caused, and to confirm my intuitions. I asked careful questions under the pseudonym "Carburetor Dung," and then waited for someone to answer. I thought I'd be buried under all the responses, but I didn't get a single sign of life, which was strange—it was as if there were some desire to wipe away bad memories. As if someone had decided what was OK to say and what was unthinkable. But who would have made this decision?

This took a lot out of me, because having exchanges with bikers, who, as Claude used to say, spent most of their time talking about how much horsepower their bikes had, brought me well out of my comfort zone. But it had to be done, because it would give me one of the most important pieces of the puzzle I was starting to put together.

I IMAGINE THE MOTORCYCLE leaving the Honda factory in Osaka in 1998, and then being transported by truck over streets and highways to a port, where it's raised up and loaded onto a cargo ship. After the customs formalities, it spends eleven days with the ship's crew, crossing stormy oceans and seas. Suez Canal. Mediterranean. Atlantic Ocean. Then it arrives in the port at Le Havre. It's unloaded in a flurry of cranes, dockworkers, seagulls, and even a picket line that's lifted at the very last moment, and stored in a warehouse while awaiting import authorization. Once the delivery slips are stamped and the customs levy paid, it's loaded onto a Renault truck, driven by a trucker who likes this, transporting motorcycles, because he's also a biker, he's a Pole, a European. Then comes the official approval I spoke of earlier. After spending some time in a warehouse near Paris, it's ordered by my brother, and delivered in autumn 1998 to a dealer in Lyon. October, November, December, January, February, March, April, May. It's kept in my brother's garage, where it's nonexistent, inoffensive, far from my daily reality. Until suddenly it arrives at my house, our house, the garage of the new house into which we were scheduled to move on Saturday, June 26, 1999. An intruder coming in through the front door.

TO SUM UP:

House, keys, garage, mother, brother, Japan, Tadao Baba, brother's holiday, Hélène, book promo.

It's all turning into quite the mess.

16

If only I hadn't done my brother a favor

THE ACT OF DOING FAVORS IS SOMETHING VERY BASIC and very interesting. Where I'm concerned, what's mine has also always been, to some degree, my brother's. Since we were kids. Give, take, give back. Some for you, some for me. We're family—we argue, we glare at each other, and sometimes we insult each other behind our backs because of the incompatibility of our political convictions. But we also love each other, which makes for a volatile mixture. Sometimes we're at each other's throats, completely exasperated, and yet we always get together for a drink on his birthday. We're able to manage that at least. We misunderstand each other, have curt exchanges, and sometimes things get really bad when we defend our points of view—we really lay into each other. And then we get together to buy a present for our parents. We try to focus on the good things and ignore the bad; we try to be tolerant.

That's the sacred word—tolerance. We tolerate each other because we're brother and sister. But is that really the best approach, to always tolerate, even when we think the other person is wrong? Not that I'm always right. I often lecture my brother like the big sister that I am, and then I feel bad for talking down to him. Then he rebukes me for my leftist moralizing: If I love immigrants so much, he asks me, why don't I go live with them? Though he's mostly stopped calling me a moralist—now he calls me a left-wing Muslim lover. He's full of barbs and cutting remarks like this. And yet despite everything, we're still brother and sister. No matter how disgusted we are with each other sometimes.

HE GETS ME DEALS on stuff because he negotiates in stores, which I'd never be able to do. I try to return such favors with advice. When he was twenty, for instance, I told him not to sign up for the war in Lebanon. I also told him he shouldn't buy stolen goods. He brings me auto parts, and I babysit his daughter on Wednesdays.

He rides a motorcycle, just like Claude did. He likes sport bikes (surprise, surprise), while Claude was content with tame vintage bikes. They used to talk about motorcycles all the time, comparing motors, gear, insurance policies. This was the turf they staked out, the terrain where they found the complicity that brothers-in-law often share.

Could I have said no when he asked to park his bike in my garage? Told him I had a bad feeling about it? But that was the point—I didn't have any bad feeling. There wasn't anything about it that bothered me. On the contrary, I was happy to do him a favor, probably because I was so happy about finally buying the house, the home we were going to work on for the summer and for an entire year beyond that. Or maybe it was because I knew he couldn't afford a house of his own. Even though he did have enough money to buy €10,000 motorcycles. Maybe I had the guilty conscience of a person with means. In fact, I know that's true. I remember telling anyone who would listen that the house belonged to everyone. It was a new kind of communism, one that included private property.

IN THE LATE AFTERNOON of Friday, June 18, my brother parked his very bulky Honda in the garage, or in other words, in what was supposed to be our future living room. He ran his chain lock, one of the strongest on the market, through the front wheel, and then wrapped it around one of the load-bearing columns. (Years later, I asked a mason if I could get rid of these columns, which were right in the middle of the future living room. Not only did I need to keep them, he said, but I'd have to reinforce the ceiling beams with stays: the garage was a former stable—you could still see the brand of the troughs on the walls—and the weight of the hayloft had caused the beams to bend over time.) No one will be stealing this, my brother said as he locked the chain—now he could enjoy his vacation in peace. He stroked the saddle of his motorcycle the same way you pat a horse's croup, with that affection he often showed for his bikes, and then reluctantly walked away. His wife drove him home in their car, and then they left for their holiday, with their daughter and without our son. He'd pick his bike up when he got back the following week.

THAT SUNDAY, WE INVITED Claude's friend Marc over to spend some time under the cherry tree with us, so we could test the garden furniture we'd just bought at the flea market. At one point Claude pointed at the motorcycle, whose sheer mass disturbed the otherwise peaceful atmosphere, and said: "That right there is forbidden. It's a real bomb. Not to be touched."

MARC WOULD LATER REPEAT these very words to me.

17

If only Claude hadn't taken my brother's motorcycle

MARC REPEATED THESE WORDS TO ME BECAUSE HE had no idea what would have made Claude change his mind. What got into him to make him ride to work, on the morning of Tuesday, June 22, on my brother's motorcycle and not on his own, his harmless Suzuki, the Suzuki he liked to ride in a "boring" way, as he used to say, which was parked in the garage in front of the primary school? What happened?

HE MUST HAVE BEEN really hesitant, because in order to ride the Honda CBR900, he'd have had to take out a temporary insurance policy. It seems to me that that's what my brother said. He also said there hadn't been many companies who wanted to take the risk of insuring his high-performance sport bike.

I think it was his way of impressing us, of emphasizing

the fact that he rode a bike that wasn't like other bikes. It was the badge of distinction that my brother no doubt needed. Or maybe it was his way of telling us that he was endangering himself, and that we should be worried for him.

He'd had to pay an enormous premium. I can't remember the name of the insurer, whom I called the week after the accident to make sure Claude had done what was required. Which would have made a big difference, at least on the financial side. Ah, it's just come back to me: La Mondiale—"Global Insurance." The agent told me that no, no one by the name of Claude S. had taken out any insurance that day. Which shocked me, because it was so unlike him.

The fact that he took that motorcycle out, when only two days earlier he'd called it a bomb that shouldn't be touched, has always struck me as an impenetrable mystery. And the fact that he didn't take out insurance simply astonishes me. Something about the whole thing isn't right. With the passing of time, I've begun to wonder if the insurance agent lied to me. After all, I didn't have any proof. It was just a telephone conversation, and back then, on landlines, there was no call history. I could have asked France Telecom for the statement, but I was too stunned to do anything like that. I took the agent at his word. I didn't even think of challenging him.

Global Insurance—it's a fitting name, since they insured motorcycles that were emblematic of the most revolting aspects of globalization.

I can't count the number of times I've tried to retrace Claude's last day. It must have gone like this:

HE WAKES UP AT seven and immediately wakes up our son. Silent breakfast with ruffled hair. Radio on in the background. Claude spills a bit of coffee like he always does. Then our son starts being his usual chatterbox self. Is Mommy coming home tonight? Is she taking the train? Will she be here by dinnertime? (I remember Claude telling me one day about how our son pined after me whenever I wasn't there. It was the same when Daddy wasn't home—he'd ask about him nonstop, wanting to know everything.) Will we go see the new house? Can I show it to Louis? Will we bring more toys over? This is another reason it's beneficial to have two parents, because each one observes the love the child feels for the other. It's the happiness of being both witness and confidant.

LONG SHOWER FOR CLAUDE with very hot water (he was already dreaming of installing a wide shower head at the new house, of water pouring down on him like a cascade). Quick shower for our son, impatient to start his day. Then they both get dressed. Claude would probably have put on the same clothes he wore the day before, same shorts, same T-shirt, though I can't be sure. He ties his shoes quickly, or maybe just puts on Velcro sandals. The hospital gave me the clothes he wore that day in a garbage bag, which I didn't dare open right away. His shirt had two ripped buttonholes, and his Perfecto jacket was torn lengthwise.

THEY RUSH DOWN THE hill because they're late, like always. Claude used to bring his son to school every morning. It was convenient because the school was right in front of the garage, I'm repeating myself, I know I'm repeating myself, but cut me some slack, I've been playing the whole thing back in my head for twenty years. They jog along the sidewalk on the left side of the road, father behind son, my son's nearly empty schoolbag (it was the end of the year) bouncing around on his back. I'd sometimes watch them going down the hill from the window of the bathroom, where I would get ready just after they left. Looking back, I realize how perfect those moments were, me at the window embracing them with my gaze, it's no exaggeration because I knew even then how beautiful it was, how lucky I was. The school was just beyond my view, so I don't know how they said goodbye to each other that morning, whether it was a quick kiss, a ruffling of the hair, or both.

And afterward?

THE SIMPLE, LOGICAL, NORMAL, and preferable option would have been to cross the street, go down some steps, walk through a little courtyard for a hundred feet or so, and open the steel door of the communal garage. Squeeze past the cars and trailers and deftly wheel out his Suzuki LS650 Savage. Put on his gloves and helmet. Close the garage. Take a few steps in the courtyard with his helmet on. (You've probably noticed how awkward bikers seem when they walk with all their gear on. Their bulky helmets make them look like aliens.) Start the bike with two or three kicks and ride to work. (The Savage may have had an electric starter, for all I know. But it doesn't matter:

I like reminiscing about how Claude used his body weight on the pedal to get the spark. I like being able to imagine him, to see his silhouette in my mind, those gestures that were both familiar and unique and that distinguished him from everyone else, that mixture of virtuosity and closeness with his machine, that graceful movement whereby he seemed to start his bike with no more than a touch and a look.) Ride to work—in other words, cover about three miles on his way downtown, cross the Rhône on the Pont Winston-Churchill, take the boulevard des Belges, then the rue Garibaldi, then get onto the boulevard Vivier-Merle right in front of the Part-Dieu train station. And arrive at the library a little before nine o'clock.

AT WHAT MOMENT DID Claude realize that he could diverge from this script? That he could simply walk the six blocks up the hill to the new house, unlock my brother's motorcycle, and take it? Was it a premeditated decision? A decision he made the day before, the night before, in the absence of my phone call?

Or did the thought strike him on the morning of June 22, after he'd dropped off his son at school, once he was bathed in the light of those first days of summer, the warmth, the smell of blooming linden trees, the intoxicating blue of the sky that would have made him feel joyful and energetic?

Did the idea hit him the moment he opened the steel door of the garage? Did he suddenly feel free because he was alone? Did the fact that his wife and son were out of sight—it's just a hypothesis—make him feel young again, young and free, with all the passion he had when he was twenty? Was it my distance from him? I'm not just talking about geographical distance. There was another distance at work here, that of a woman who was becoming more and more involved in the literary world in Paris, which he must have begun to feel, and which was bound to influence him, even if only in a tiny way.

Or was he simply in the grasp of a childish, archaic, and visceral desire to drive an enormous machine, to treat himself to a feeling he'd remember forever, an injection of adrenaline like the fix you sometimes get from rock and roll, a fix he'd never outgrown?

It was now or never: Claude could test-drive this motorcycle the way some people test-drive cars with huge engines, making the motor purr and the tires squeal. Wasn't this the dream conveyed by every action movie in the history of cinema? With their heroes who devote themselves to high-speed chases that are as simple as they are joyful (for both driver and spectator), and their universal stories of speed, risk-taking, and virility (once again), stories that changed dramatically with the arrival of the internal combustion engine and its famous carburetor, the one that has taken over my entire inner being. Destroyed carburetors. And carburetors that destroy.

AT EIGHT THIRTY ON that Tuesday morning, Claude suddenly feels the desire for adventure, a desire that leads him to a series of transgressions. OK, maybe it's not Mad

Max—it's slightly less spectacular—but considering that it was school hours, it's still quite the wild escapade.

Elegant, refined, discreet, modest Claude: this was his dark side, his B side. Which I also loved.

Other people are always a mystery, and trying to figure out what goes on in their minds leads to years of thinking, speaking, and writing. How does a reasonable and predictable person—a person you might simply call an adult—become capricious, transgressive? What turns a good bourgeois citizen—a good father, someone who takes out a mortgage at the bank—into a punk rocker at the very next moment, someone ready to take everything apart, to *muck it all up*?

SOMETHING'S NOT RIGHT. DON'T do it.

Don't walk up that hill. Can't you sense the risks?

CLAUDE WALKS THE SIX hundred yards (I just checked on Google Maps) up to the new house (the Merciers' house) with his helmet in hand and his Perfecto jacket slung across his back. It's a steep hill. He walks with his right leg slightly tucked in, something I noticed when I was seventeen, the first time he picked me up at high school on his motorcycle. It's hard to climb a hill as steep as the Montée du Belvédère, but he's determined. He struggles a little—maybe he even stops and catches his breath—but he doesn't stop. I can't quite make him out in my mind. He's blurry.

Something's not quite right.

HE UNLOCKS THE HONDA CBR900 that's waiting in the garage, in that dark and inhospitable space that's not yet lit up by the bay window I installed years later.

He straddles the motorcycle, probably finding it difficult to maneuver its 403 pounds (three times his weight). Even though Tadao Baba did all he could to produce an ultralight engine, you still have to know how to handle it.

He starts it up. An electric starter. I've checked.

But how did he get the keys? (I'm not even going to mention the registration.)

The keys. I insist on asking. How did he get them? I don't remember my brother . . . Unless . . .

IF I'D PHONED THE night before, from my Parisian sofa (yes, *my* Parisian sofa), would something in my voice have prevented him from taking that motorcycle?

THESE ARE PROBABLY THE wrong questions. But it seems I can't find the right ones.

18

If only Stephen King had died on Saturday, June 19, 1999

I'VE TRIED TO HUNT DOWN SOME EVENT, SOME news item, some human interest story that Claude might have heard about in the days leading up to the accident, something that might have deterred him and prevented him from going to fetch the Honda. What would it have taken for Claude to be on his guard? What revelation, what headline in the papers, might have made him smell the danger floating in the air that day?

I'VE TRIED TO TAKE note of everything that happened in the world the day before June 22, 1999, the day before that, and that day before that as well, something that might have made him think about our fragility, that might have scared him, petrified him so much that he wouldn't even dare to jaywalk. But I didn't find what I was looking for. All I found were articles reflecting the somewhat boring state of the planet at the very end of the twentieth century.

ALL I FOUND WERE unsurprising sports results, like Australia prevailing over Pakistan in cricket, boring economic stories, such as Elf losing the battle to take over Saga Petroleum, or news about international politics; I found stories about public health inspectors and doctors who were protesting, even back then, for bigger hospital budgets. I saw that the writer Mario Soldati had died, which I'd forgotten, Mario Soldati, wow, that should have had some kind of impact, but he died at the age of ninety-two of natural causes, which was hardly shocking, it wouldn't have made you think twice. I saw that Jacques Chirac had just scored a fifty-eight percent favorability rating in the latest IFOP poll, that the G7 meeting in Cologne had decided to partially forgive the debt of the poorest countries, and that a few journalists had been imprisoned in Iran.

I WAS DISAPPOINTED. I wanted to find a reason to retroactively stop the course of events, even after all this time, and give history a chance to unfold differently. Surely there was one item in all these news stories, in this glut of information, that could have stopped Claude in his tracks. While flipping through a twenty-year-old issue of *Le Nouvel Observateur*, I came across a story about the premature death of Élie Kakou on June 19, 1999. Élie Kakou, that sounded familiar, I wanted to find out more. He was thirty-nine years old, almost the same age as

Claude. But he died of AIDS. Of course, I'd forgotten—Élie Kakou, it was all coming back to me, he was Madame Sarfati in the famous sketch on that TV show, Claude and I had watched it with his family, it made everyone laugh, he talked about how they'd left everything behind "over there," the French people who'd come from Algeria like Claude and his parents, they'd arrived in France "as naked as the day they were born," the same expression his mother used, with the exact same accent, the one that was so often ridiculed. Those memories came flooding back, even if the comedian's death wasn't the event I was looking for. I stopped everything to watch Élie Kakou sketches on my computer—it was like I was glued to my desk in the little back room that had become my office—and I smiled as he did the kibbutz scene, I clicked and I laughed, that damn Élie Kakou, he must have really suffered. I went from video to video, it was easier than writing, and even though it wasn't really relevant to the matter at hand, at least it brought back pleasant memories of Claude. I went down quite the YouTube rabbit hole, and by the end I realized that I was just as in love as I had been twenty years ago.

I didn't give up—I kept looking for that one event. There just had to be some minor news item, some scandal or tragedy, that could have influenced Claude that day, some beating of a butterfly's wing that could have ended up affecting him. The closure of the Chernobyl nuclear reactor wouldn't have made any difference, and nor would the record-breaking week at the Paris stock exchange, or the indictment of Claude Évin for involuntary manslaughter in the contaminated blood affair.

I was getting annoyed. I wanted to force the news outlets to spit out some dramatic event that would eventually have made its way into Claude's consciousness and prevented him from walking to the Merciers' house.

I was sure the right piece of news existed, so I kept racking my brain. After my long break watching Élie Kakou videos, I started flipping through old datebooks and newspapers, specifically the issues of *Le Monde* from 1999 that I'd brought along in the move (Claude had published several articles that year), and which I kept within easy reach, thinking I might find a trace there of Claude's last days and, more broadly, of the mood of the time, some atmosphere that would link me to him and keep him in my memory. I also kept copies of *Libération*, and every issue of *Les Inrockuptibles*, *Rock & Folk*, and *New Musical Express*, all those magazines that were his daily bread.

That day, as was often the case back then, I didn't write at all. I just flipped through newspapers, watched videos, paced around the house, and tried once more to halt the passage of time. I was on a mad quest, and I had no idea where it was going.

AND THEN I DISCOVERED an article about what had happened to Stephen King three days before Claude's accident, in other words Saturday, June 19, 1999, at around four thirty in the afternoon, while he was taking his daily walk in the Maine countryside. I suddenly remembered how it had rattled us. I'd forgotten all about it: Stephen King had been hit by a minivan and thrown into a ditch. They found him in bad shape, unconscious, with multiple fractures and a punctured lung.

Claude liked everything Stephen King wrote, but above all he was crazy about *The Shining*, to which he often alluded when we bought our relatively isolated house. The music from the film had made such an impression on him that he assigned it to his students (he sometimes worked as an adjunct professor here and there).

When we found out about Stephen King's accident, we tried to remember which of his books we owned, but we couldn't check because we'd already boxed up all our books and brought them to the new house.

This is the news item that could have dissuaded Claude from putting himself in danger, if only it had been a little more serious. It wasn't enough for Stephen King to be severely wounded. He would have had to die.

He'd been evacuated by helicopter, and journalists from all over the world rushed to the hospital where he was being treated. The surgeons had come close to amputating one of his legs. He'd come within an inch of his life and was badly shaken, but he was alive. Which makes all the difference: it reminds us that death is always lurking somewhere, but it gives us a kind of thrill, electrifying us rather than making us stop and think. A little later, I learned (on my own, of course) that the painkillers they prescribed him plunged him back into the addictions of his youth, and that he developed a fetishistic relationship with the number 19, because the accident happened on June 19, just as I would soon begin to anxiously venerate the number 22.

He managed to pull through, merely brushing up against the death that would no doubt have led Claude to think twice. And I think I was angry at Stephen King for coming out the other side, for not doing what I needed him to do.

19

If only that Tuesday morning had been rainy

THE IDEA NEVER OCCURRED TO ME THAT THAT Tuesday morning could have been rainy. Sometimes all it takes to make life go in a different direction is one little thing. Something as simple and trivial as the weather. It's unsettling to think about it. To tell the truth, I'd never considered it. Because you always take for granted that June is bursting with warmth and light, especially in Lyon, where the temperature sometimes rises with dizzying speed around the summer solstice. With the constant threat of storms toward the end of the day, as the organizers of the Nuits de Fourvière festival can attest. I remember being at a Tindersticks concert during the festival where it rained so hard that Stuart Staples, the lead singer, must have been happy to be wearing that thick tweed jacket that makes him look so British, and that he rarely takes off onstage. It got so cold all at once, and the rain was so heavy, that I bought a plastic rain cape from a hawker who was walking up and down the steps of the amphitheater, and which I still keep in my bag for when I go hiking. It's my Tindersticks rain cape. Claude would have loved the idea.

The idea that June 22, 1999, could have been a rain-soaked, chilly, and frankly terrible day had never occurred to me. For once the rain would have brought something good to my life—it would have blessed us, it would have surprised me when I got off the train from Paris, it would have made my hair frizzy, and would have made me hurry to the bus shelter, where I'd have caught the last 38 to get home. I would have arrived soaking wet and in a bad mood, but I'd have put my feet up on the table, and Claude would have heated up the meal he'd prepared, maybe chili con carne, which was one of his classics, though then again he might not have had time to make a big meal right in the middle of a move.

WHAT WOULD CLAUDE HAVE done if it had rained that Tuesday morning?

HE DEFINITELY WOULDN'T HAVE gone through the effort of climbing up to the Merciers' house to unlock the Honda from the pole. It's far more likely that after dropping his son off at school, he'd have looked up at the sky, smelling the air as he took shelter under an umbrella and turning toward the south and then the west, because that's how you check the weather when you live in Lyon, you scan the horizon toward the Rhône valley and the Feyzin refinery, looking for a ray of light in the distance that might be a sign that the sun will come out. The sun will come out, the words remind me of that song by the group Marc Seberg, which Claude often hummed, and of their lead singer, Philippe Pascal, also a child of the Algerian War, who just took his own life.

Back then, before the end of the last century, we didn't check the weather on our cell phones. We'd look at the sky and at those two cardinal points, making haphazard calculations based on the direction of the wind and the shape of the clouds. And we'd also say a little prayer.

Claude would have gazed up at the sky. He did the same thing every morning when he opened the bedroom window, sticking his hand outside in a silly gesture that made us both laugh, as if this would allow him to judge both the temperature and the reliability of the forecast. Every morning he'd test the air like this, apprehensively, as if his life depended on it, and in a way it did, because riding a motorcycle in wet conditions is a lot harder than riding on dry Algerian roads, notwithstanding their steep drop-offs. I'm saying this as a reminder that he wasn't really from here, that his presence above the forty-fifth parallel was a mistake, and if the winds of history, as he liked to say, hadn't brought him to the north shore of the Mediterranean, he would never have had to worry about what we call "weather" in temperate countries. He'd have lived his life in shirtsleeves in the eternally warm air; he'd have walked barefoot and ridden without a helmet. Instead of wearing boots and shivering from November to May.

IF IT HAD RAINED that morning, Claude would have crossed the street that leads to the garage, stopped to think for a minute, sighed, hunched up his shoulders, and absentmindedly scratched his three-day-old beard. He'd undoubtedly have ridden his Suzuki Savage to work. It's true that he'd have considered taking the bus that stops three blocks from there, since after all it would have brought him right to the office—he wouldn't even have needed to transfer. But as I think about it now, I realize that this is just one more of those fantasies I love to indulge in. Taking the bus was an ordeal for Claude. He couldn't stand the pace, the etiquette, the ceremony of it all. He hated schedules, tickets, and following the crowd without being able to act. He also hated being vertical, standing up and holding the bar; I think I'm right to say he found it annoying being tall. The bus wasn't for him. Motorcycles, on the other hand, were perfectly adapted to the urban life that he cherished; they provided an escape route, a feeling of independence that reassured him. Walking, whether it was strolling in the city or hiking in the mountains, wasn't his strong suit. He felt best on two wheels—that's how he found his center of gravity.

It all started with bicycles, when he was just a child, which makes me think of that photo of him riding a tricycle on the patio in Algiers. When he arrived in France, his parents got him a kids' bike, and then, when he was a teenager, he bought himself a used BMX, which he used to fly down hills and do tricks in front of the high-rises in his neighborhood. Soon he was even doing risky maneuvers in the streets, according to his friend Alain, who lived in the same building in Rillieux-la-Pape, and who spent evenings with him listening to records. Then Claude got his motorcycle license, and it was a whole other story.

IF IT HAD RAINED on the morning of June 22, Claude would never have walked up the hill, where the water would have been streaming down. He wouldn't have dreamed of getting his shoes wet (he loved his shoes so much . . . I'm just realizing the hospital never gave them back to me), he'd never have waded through the channels of water to get to the Merciers' house. He'd have known he might run the risk of losing control of the CBR900, which would have defeated the purpose—the whole reason he rode was for the pleasure it gave him. It just wouldn't have been worth it to take the bike out in hostile conditions, with drops of water forming little furrows on the visor of his helmet and blinding him.

No, he'd have done the exact same thing he did each day: opened the garage door, weaved through the other bikes until he reached his Suzuki, taken his rain suit out of one of the leather saddlebags fastened to the back of the bike, and reluctantly pulled it on, because that's how you put on rain suits and boot covers, with frustration and even with sorrow. He'd have done up the zippers as far as they go, realizing he wouldn't feel anything at all on the ride to work, not euphoria, not peace, not even a sense that something unexpected might happen, which is the very opposite of what you expect when you straddle your motorbike on a

June morning. It would have been hard just to move in that plastic outfit that he hated, which he'd bought at the used motorcycle goods market that takes place on the first Sunday of every month in Neuville-sur-Saône, where we went from time to time when we were looking for an accessory or a part that was too expensive in the stores. And also for the sheer pleasure of hunting for bargains in the stalls, and of fleetingly being part of a community.

CLAUDE WOULD HAVE SHIFTED into first, gotten onto the road with water spraying all around him, and ridden at half mast, as it were, to the library, where he'd have arrived in a pitiful state. None of his colleagues would be jealous of him, and not a single girl would notice him as he walked by, since every trace of his normally cool look would have disappeared. He'd have locked his bike in his reserved spot in the parking lot, and then continued by foot in his dripping rain gear, stopping at the caretaker's lodge to ask if he could leave it to dry somewhere in the hallway. They'd have made a few chummy remarks about the weather, it's not supposed to be like this on the second day of summer, thankfully it didn't rain the night before for World Music Day. They'd have betted it wouldn't last, and in fact it wouldn't have lasted, two hours later the atmospheric pressure would have risen and the rain would have slowed at the same time as the north wind would have picked up slightly, a wind that was light and hence perfect for dissipating the clouds, and the sun would have come out, the light would have been lively, dazzling, the swifts would have come back, flying in endless circles, their cries echoing off the facades of buildings and entering through the bay window of Claude's office, which he'd have opened to welcome in the summer.

But the weather was beautiful on that Tuesday, June 22, as beautiful as you might expect in early summer. And so Claude walked up to the Merciers' house.

20

If only Claude had listened to "Don't Panic" by Coldplay, and not "Dirge" by Death in Vegas, before leaving the office

CLAUDE ARRIVED AT WORK ON THE ENORMOUS BLACK-and-gold Honda, and the caretaker in the lodge of the enormous ship that is the Bibliothèque Municipale de Lyon whistled with admiration and a bit of astonishment. "Are you ready for the Twenty-Four Hours of Le Mans?" he joked, mixing things up a bit.

After a modest and (as he liked to joke) somewhat directionless beginning to his professional life—he'd gotten a job in the clearing service of the Bank of France, driven by the need to support himself financially after his military service—Claude found out about a new position in the music section of the library, where he spent a lot of time as a patron (a word he hated), often bringing me along on Saturdays.

You have to remember that this was before the internet, when the only music formats were CDs and vinyl, along with cassettes for copying them. You couldn't listen to what you wanted when you wanted. You had to wait for Bernard Lenoir to play new songs on the radio, or for rock critics like Arnaud Viviant, JD Beauvallet, Bayon, or Michka Assayas to give you guidance. We used to buy a lot of music, in shops on the rue Mercière or the slopes of the Croix-Rousse, where we spent large amounts of time and money, sometimes ordering prohibitively expensive imports that took weeks to arrive from the US or the UK, which we'd wait for with bated breath. And we hung out at the library, where we could borrow three records a week.

Our happiness came from these limitations on our choices, and the fear of making a mistake. Or the discoveries we made by chance, at the music stores but also at the library, when the records we'd been counting on were already loaned out. Our happiness came from the desire we felt, which was heightened by the wait. Our happiness came from what was scarce, what was rare.

Claude really wanted the position. He began studying the history of music, both classical and popular, to prepare for the civil service examination. He wanted to leave the bank and immerse himself body and soul in the music scene. By dint of some miracle, he landed the job, and eventually he became the head of his unit, all without having to get rid of his Chelsea boots and his Perfecto jacket. This would have been unthinkable at the bank, where his boss had asked him to wear suits instead of sneakers.

AT THE DISCO, AS he called the library's music section, Claude spent his time building a catalog, listening to music, turning a vinyl collection into a CD collection, wondering whether he should create a section dedicated to rap (which was booming) and another for electronic music, debating how he should categorize this or that album (was it house or jungle?), reorganizing categories or getting rid of them entirely if he decided they were out of date. He also had to plan team meetings, deal with—or at least not avoid—personnel management (which wasn't his strong suit), and come to terms with a hierarchy in which he stood at the top. He sometimes took leave for training sessions on various currents of rock in places like Bordeaux, Arles, and Nantes. He listened to albums at home in the evening, took notes, shared his discoveries with me. It was one of his reasons for living: discovering, unearthing, listening, listening again, and passing on.

Among the moments that have stayed in my memory is the time he arrived with Dominique A's first album, *La Fossette*, when he ordered me not to move, in other words to sit on the little sofa in the kitchen and listen without any distractions (I remember his command like it was yesterday). Our shoulders touched and we looked at each other in amazement as we heard the first notes of "Courage des oiseaux," that song that, of all the songs we liked, will always remain our song, our rallying cry, our secret code, just as it became the symbol of an entire generation. I still remember how that evening, after dinner, after we put our son to bed (he wasn't even eighteen months old yet), we listened to Dominique A's album over and over, amazed and wildly excited.

IT WAS A TUESDAY. It would soon be 4:00 p.m., according to the clock on the library wall. There were a few CDs sitting on Claude's desk, which he wanted to listen to one last time. Alain Bashung, Daft Punk, Coldplay, Death in Vegas, Placebo, Radiohead, Massive Attack. He kept an eye on the clock. He had to choose one final song, one that wouldn't be too long, before leaving work, nodding to his colleagues as he slipped out quietly. One more for the road—the expression was never more fitting. The one that would allow him to walk through the door of the library at exactly the right moment, so he wouldn't arrive late to the school, where his son was waiting for him (where his son wasn't waiting for him).

HE WAS AN EXPERT in that practice we're all familiar with, the final email, the final phone call, the final customer, the last act of the day, which we judge according to how much time it will take. All the while knowing that it will inevitably make us late. In an instant you go from being ahead to being behind, because as everyone knows, the time you spend on the job—especially since the arrival of email, which still wasn't that important in 1999—is like a river overflowing its banks, and there's always something at the end of the day, some meeting to fit in, some emergency to take care of, some final stroke of genius, that ends up making you late. The phone always rings right when you're about to go home.

In other words, no one ever leaves early anymore. It just doesn't happen. Even in branches of the civil service like a public library.

THE SHORTEST SONG, AT 3'27", was Coldplay's "Don't Panic," which had just come out, and which was in the box that had just been delivered from the record store on the rue Mercière. But Claude wanted to hear "Dirge," by Death in Vegas (he would never see the cult Levi's commercial in which it featured a few months later), which comes in at 5'44". It was a dilemma over two minutes. In other words, nothing—it's laughable even to think about it. What's two minutes in the course of a life, or even in the course of a day? Two minutes—you'd just need to turn the song off before the end, or drive a bit faster on the way home, or not, because there's no use rushing in the city, the traffic lights dictate your speed, as Claude knew, because for a long time he'd gotten around by bicycle (the bicycle that I still have in the backyard), and he'd noticed that it took the same time whether he was riding a bicycle or a motorbike, other than the hill on the way home, you just had to "deal with it," as he loved saying, because the expression reminded him of the working-class jargon they used in his family, a family that had been tossed about from city to city since their re-patriation from Algeria.

So even on the CBR900, it would take him just under fifteen minutes, and even if he arrived after the school bell had already sounded, it wouldn't be the end of the world. As I've already mentioned, every parent was at some point the last one to arrive, especially if he worked, and every parent knew that another parent would stay behind if he was late, that no child would ever be left alone on the sidewalk. Of course, the person waiting might get worried and even a bit annoyed, but it all worked out in the end: bring our kid over to your place for dinner, and your kid can come play at our house next week.

SO CLAUDE DECIDED TO listen to "Dirge," though I have to admit that I'm not certain (I'm relying on what Eric told me, since his desk was only a few feet away, and he saw Claude put the CD back in its case), I'm just putting forth hypotheses to alleviate the feeling of emptiness that takes hold of me whenever I try to imagine that final day. He chose "Dirge" so that he'd be slightly late, thus creating the kind of minor adrenaline rush that gives spice to life. Nothing strange in that: time, for men, seems to be a constant series of delays. Ignition delays, I almost wrote.

I LISTENED TO "DIRGE" nonstop for months, obsessed by it, as if I were being pulled toward it, the song and also the band, Death in Vegas, a British band founded by Richard Fearless. I know every second of that haunting song that begins with a guitar and a woman's voice, continues with the entrance of a distorted synthesizer, takes things up a notch when a dirty guitar sound appears, supported by drums that soon move into the foreground, all of it absorbing the original guitar and voice that nonetheless remain. I listened again and again, experiencing every one of the song's layers as they increase, intensify, and give form to those few repetitive notes (fa, mi, re, fa, do, re) that adorn an intensity that's impossible to interrupt. I challenge anyone to stop "Dirge" before the end, that's what I've always said, it would be like pausing sex right when you're getting into it, turning on the light right when you're about to climax. You feel like you're taking part in the saturation and the trembling; the notes, tenuous and restrained at first, soon climb in increments, bringing you further and further along in a sort of addictive tranquility, a flow at once psychedelic and punk, a thick fabric that you immerse yourself in without ever wanting to leave. It's so good.

AND THAT'S THE PROBLEM.
   Just leave! Turn it off! Don't let yourself be seduced.
   Grab your stuff and go.

I WONDER WHAT CLAUDE would have written about it if he'd reviewed it for the newspaper, what he could have said about that song of just under six minutes without simply writing *la la la, la la la*. He often confessed that he found it impossible to write about music, and that he was amazed when he read work as inspired as that of Greil Marcus or Lester Bangs, those legendary critics who were able to give rock the prestige and respectability it deserved.

I admit I was trying to surprise him one last time with the lines I just wrote about the song. I'd like to think he's smiling right now. About my labored seriousness, my clear conviction.

CLAUDE WROTE WELL, AND I found his talent really attractive. Sometimes he asked me to read his work when he wasn't sure everything was clear, or when he wondered about the appropriateness of a slightly lewd metaphor. He wrote his articles on a Canon word processor at home in the evenings; I think he then printed them out and brought them to the newspaper. His floppy disks sat at the bottom of boxes for a long time before I dared to look at them; I imagine they were from later, when Claude bought his first computer. I'm mixing things up as time goes by.

IT WAS 3:55 P.M. when Claude finally slipped toward the exit. He hadn't taken the time to say goodbye to his colleagues, who knew all about his legendary ability to be late, and didn't begrudge him leaving a little early twice a week. He pulled on his jacket as he opened the door. I imagine him juggling his backpack, keys, helmet, and gloves, trying to hold it all and still have a finger free to push the button of the elevator that would bring him to the ground floor. He was hoping that the elevator wouldn't take long to arrive (it often took several minutes), that it wasn't blocked on one of the higher floors, for example in the rare books section where Guy worked—Guy, with whom he'd had lunch that day, and who gave me all the details about his final meal, as well as other things I wasn't aware of.

CLAUDE MADE IT DOWN to the ground floor and said hi to the caretaker, who may have been keeping an eye on the Honda—that's something I never asked about—and who watched Claude start that monster of a motorcycle (I have no idea whether the caretaker was amazed or unsettled), pushing the electric button after pulling on his helmet and putting his new backpack over his shoulders, the backpack in which I'd find, once they gave his things back to me, the huge steel lock, CDs by Coldplay and Massive Attack, two *Quick et Flupke* comic books he'd borrowed for his son, and an issue of *Les Inrockuptibles* from June 1999 with an image from Larry Clark's new film *Another Day in Paradise* on the cover. He turned the throttle and revved the engine but stayed where he was, to show the caretaker, who was behind his glass, or rather standing on his doorstep in the warm June air, that he had serious power under the fairing, and also to show him that he could also speak his language, that he could talk about more than just music, he could be something other than an intellectual working in a library, he could joke around with the guy in the lodge who probably didn't listen to the same music as him, or read the same books, and who spent his days craning his neck to watch a little television screwed high up on his wall, which would undoubtedly compress his vertebrae and give him chronic pain. Claude revved it again two or three times as he tried to maneuver the 403-pound bike and point it toward the exit. He made sure he wasn't forgetting anything and then nodded toward the caretaker, who responded with a thumbs-up. See you tomorrow. *Ciao amigo.* See you tomorrow.

IT WAS EXACTLY 4:00 p.m. For once in his life, he was almost early.

21

If only Claude hadn't forgotten his three hundred francs in the Société Générale cash machine

BUT NOT SO EARLY AFTER ALL, BECAUSE CLAUDE
had to make an unplanned stop, which would divert him
slightly from his normal route. Guy told me this little anec-
dote a few weeks after the accident, and I didn't know how
to interpret it. Claude had taken money out earlier that
day before going for lunch with Guy at Tout Va Bien, a
restaurant on the corner of the cours Lafayette, which has
since closed, and he'd forgotten his three hundred francs
in the cash machine of the Société Générale. He realized
when he went to pay for his daily special and coffee, and
swore that it was true, which made Guy laugh, because
everyone knew how forgetful Claude was, how he was
always losing things, like his office keys, his colleagues
always made fun of him for that, the keys that open the
main door of the library, which is why people often gathered

in the hallway at opening time, waiting for someone to unlock the door.

In the end Claude paid with his debit card (it was the end of the month, and he'd used up all the restaurant credit he was entitled to in his job), but not before checking the pockets of his jacket, which he never took off, even in the middle of the summer, because he kept everything important in his pockets—wallet, cash, various sets of keys, sunglasses, and no doubt other stuff as well. And that wasn't the only reason he so rarely removed his Perfecto jacket, as he confessed to me one day when I teased him about it a little. He wasn't very bulky, he said, so he felt vulnerable, because he didn't fit the ideal of a man with a broad and muscular chest. And that's what I loved about him, that slender build, that sharp profile, that angular beauty. He wanted to stop at the bank after he left Tout Va Bien, but he didn't have enough time. He'd pop in later that afternoon on his way home.

IT WAS FOUR O'CLOCK, and Claude still had to make that detour before going to pick up his son at school. It would only take a few minutes, because the Société Générale was on a nearby cross street, a one-way street in the wrong direction, it's true, but only three blocks away. I just checked.

He parked between two cars and took off his helmet so he wouldn't scare the employee who had to unlock the door when he rang the bell. He was attended to by a young man in a short-sleeved shirt, the very man Claude had been when he was twenty, whom he probably thought back on in horror. The young man smiled at him, which soon became awkward because Claude didn't return his smile—he wasn't being mean, just straightforward, projecting confidence while hoping that the cash machine had swallowed his bills before anyone could take them, and that the bank would give him his money back without any fuss. He had to fill out a form, which meant waiting several long minutes at the window, talking through the grill, looking for his account number, his routing number, his bank code, searching his pockets for his checkbook so he could find all these numbers he didn't know by heart, trying to write them down with a pen that didn't work, starting over because he'd put too many zeros, and then waiting for the teller, who was now on the phone, to come back to him. The teller had to take the form, stamp it, tear off a copy, give it to Claude, and record the request. Which would all take longer than Claude had anticipated, and would thus make him late, even though to that point he'd been making good time. The whole business with the form had put him behind schedule, which made his muscles tense up just a little, as he realized he had to hurry, he had no more room for error.

I NEVER KNEW IF they gave Claude his money right there at the counter after he filled out the form, which was a sworn statement that he hadn't touched the three hundred francs that the cash machine had issued a few hours earlier, because there wasn't any cash among the items returned to me by the hospital. It would never have crossed my mind to ask about it when I picked his things up because I only found out about it later, but even if I'd known, I'm not sure I'd have had enough energy to open my mouth and dispute what they were telling me, or even to raise the slightest doubt. I remember that I was still in shock, which is probably why I never asked about his watch either.

I'M NOT SURE CLAUDE did actually stop at the bank as he'd told Guy he would. Maybe he thought it was already too late. I have no proof, and in any case it doesn't matter. I never thought about checking to see if the three hundred francs had been debited from his account, even though I knew his password, I still remember it: 2599. I could have found out immediately. 2599. Or I could have checked the bank statement that arrived in the mailbox at the beginning of July.

22

If only the light hadn't turned red

CLAUDE HURRIED OUT OF THE SOCIÉTÉ GÉNÉRALE and got back into the flow of traffic leading to the boulevard des Brotteaux, which in turn leads to the boulevard des Belges as it goes past the Parc de la Tête-d'Or, where the mansions and luxury apartments come one after another, and where there's not a single bakery or café on any corner. He went at a moderate speed, completely unlike the ride he'd taken that morning on the Lyon ring road (I haven't discussed this yet, it would have made me lose my thread, and also I wasn't really ready to write about it), where he tested the bike's speed, handling, brakes, and his own ability to take the reins of such a powerful machine for the first time in his life. That's what Guy told me after the accident. When Claude picked up the Honda at the Merciers' house, or rather at his house, he decided to see what it had in its belly, getting it up to 125 miles per hour on the ring road, it was on that bit before Vaulx-en-Velin that doesn't have any radar, he got into the passing lane and burst into the rearview mirrors of all the motorists like a rocket (weren't there any traffic jams that morning?), and then bragged about it when he got to work, how he'd reconnected with the energy of his youth and touched the darkness that was buried deep inside of him, which no doubt contained a violence that had lain dormant since he'd been snatched from war-torn Algeria as a child. Or maybe (I can't be sure) he just wanted to commune with those words of Lou Reed, "Live fast, die young," smiling all the while with that crooked grin that was half angel and half devil, a smile that could make you fall for him at the drop of a hat—I can see him now with that rictus that made me crazy for him. Or simply crazy.

When I think back now about how he flew down the ring road, it somehow makes sense. After all, he wasn't going to borrow the Honda just so he could drive to work, stopping at traffic lights and getting stuck behind buses pulling out in front of him. He wasn't going to hold back—he wanted to push the motor as far as it would go, hear it roar, and feel that reactor with its almost atomic power between his legs, pushing him forward at the speed of lightning.

BUT THE TEST RIDE was over. Now he was riding home calmly at the end of the day, already getting into his evening routine, thinking about what he'd do when he got back to the apartment. With the satisfaction you always feel when the work day is done. He'd be home again, relaxing in his cozy space, shut away and protected, with no witnesses to his regression. Because we always regress when we walk through the door. For Claude, it meant eating Côte d'Or chocolate, or Ovomaltine bars he bought in packs of four, while standing in front of the cupboard; it meant drinking milk straight from the bottle while crouching in front of the fridge and swapping his shoes for slippers, which immediately made him look far less cool. It meant opening his backpack to take out the records he planned to play and the book he'd borrowed, *A Confederacy of Dunces*, which Guy had recommended to him. I'd find it in his backpack later.

The test ride was over, he was on his way home from work, and now everything would calm down. He'd take the motorbike and lock it to the post once and for all. It makes me think of that very angry song by Dominique A, "Le Travail," from his album *La mémoire neuve*, which he might have listened to during the day, and which I've listened to so often, searching for a hidden meaning, that it's become meaningless for me. That one line: "I was on my way home from work, and no one was waiting for me."

THE STATS DON'T LIE: two out of every three serious accidents take place on the daily commute, those short, repetitive trips that we think are risk-free because they're like second nature. It's the lack of adventure that kills: the absence of risk itself becomes the greatest risk. When I was told about the accident that evening when I got home from Paris, I didn't imagine for a second that it could be serious, since it seemed impossible that anything so dramatic could happen on a routine commute. Which is why my response was selfish and a bit coarse: having an accident right before a move, that's not very smart, it's going to make everything more complicated. I was rather annoyed.

CLAUDE HAD ALWAYS OWNED motorbikes. He bought a Yamaha 125 when he was eighteen and living with his parents in the housing development in Rillieux-la-Pape. He would drive by my building while leaning into a ninety-degree turn, mischievously throttling down and then quickly up, no doubt to attract my attention—did he know (I never told him) that as soon as I heard the sound of the engine I'd rush over to my bedroom window? Then he got a very sleek Kawasaki 650, which was stolen in broad daylight in front of the Opéra de Lyon, in the little street where we rented that first apartment that we were evicted from. Then it was a Yamaha XT500, "the big thumper," as he called it, which he cherished, and on which we crisscrossed all the roads of the region, until we got into an accident on the way to Villard-de-Lans on May 10, 1981, which left me with a head injury and a loss of consciousness (I couldn't remember whom I'd voted for), leading to a brief stay in the University Hospital in Grenoble. After that he stuck to his bicycle for a while, before buying his first new motorcycle, the Suzuki LS650 Savage that I've talked about so much, which he appreciated for its charm and its great handling, and which I had to get rid of—I sold it in the summer of 1999 to a young man from Chambéry (I never told him the reason I had to part with it). And then there were all those bikes I've forgotten, which were stolen one after another (leading to several disagreements with insurance companies). He'd talk about them with his friends, and I'd catch the occasional snippet of these conversations, which allowed me to pick up a bit of that peculiar and fascinating vocabulary. He'd also talk about his aversion to cars, how he was the kind of man who didn't like to weigh himself down and who rebelled against every kind of subservience, especially the subservience of traffic jams. And let's not even talk about his hatred of highway toll machines, which he considered insulting, and which he always sped through without paying.

CLAUDE RODE DOWN THE boulevard normally, you might say, weaving between vehicles, as bikers have always done, since they can't bear the idea of waiting behind others, since the idea of being behind cars has always driven them crazy. He behaved like an impatient bee, buzzing down the left side of the street, zigzagging slowly through traffic, taking liberties that probably annoyed those around him, tailing people and then flying past them. He was having fun, that's what I imagine, or more like what I hope, enjoying the bike's smooth accelerations, the fruit of the carburetor designed by Tadao Baba; he was champing at the bit, but his pleasure was limited by the cars, which at that time of the day move smoothly, at least, along a stretch of road where the speed limit is forty miles per hour.

He was fluttering about like a bee gathering pollen. Or

lisping, you might say, because the motor of a sport bike never sounds right when it's being ridden in stops and starts. Claude barely needed his right hand on the accelerator. But then again, what do I know, maybe he tore through the neighborhood like a shooting star, thumbing his nose at the traffic, in a long, straight line (with a few swerves here and there) on the left-hand side, hugging the white line (it's just a symbol after all), passing the 38, the bus I always took—and that I still take—on my way home from the train station, from my adventures in Paris, the bus that crawls along at a snail's pace before letting me off halfway up the Montée de la Boucle, on the other side of the Rhône, where we were living.

THE RHÔNE FORMS THE border between the sixth arrondissement and the Croix-Rousse neighborhood, where our apartment and our son's school were located. The river is large and luminous at that point, just upstream from the city center, just a little ways past the Saint-Clair waterfall, where it cascades in a foam that's often thick (it depends on the time of year) and that's always a shade of blue that's almost white, recalling its source in the glaciers. The Rhône's water level starts to rise in June, but swimming is prohibited, and fishing as well. You can't eat the fish because they're contaminated with PCBs. I remember we talked about it once at dinner, the pollution in the Rhône, that disturbing cocktail of nitrates, heavy metals, and pesticides for which we've invented a new term, PCBs, which at the time was on the front page of the local newspapers.

I'M PUTTING OFF THE moment when I'll have to bring Claude's journey to a halt, when I'll have to let the light turn red. I'm talking about the traffic light in front of the Musée Guimet, which will henceforth play a decisive role. For the moment I'm speaking about PCBs and those little impromptu beaches frequented by young nature lovers who warm themselves in the rays of the sun reflecting off the river, by boys who like to meet there, by students who seclude themselves in the trees to roll joints and spend the evening around a fire, strumming their guitars and beating their djembe drums, which you can hear all the way to the Croix-Rousse hill.

I'M TRYING NOT TO let the light turn red, because if it had stayed green a second longer, Claude would have just carried on, without any problems, not just his commute but his life as well. We wouldn't even think about that day, which would have been just like all the others, neither remarkable nor memorable. It wouldn't have given rise to any questions, and certainly not any stories like this one. It would simply have been a normal day, a day with all the different facets of the season, a day of short sleeves, warm breezes, with an afternoon like silk, a day just before school lets out for summer, just before the great liberation, and also just before our move, just before that new life we knew was finally about to unfold. This was how I saw things, in any case, and maybe I was the only one who saw them this way. I imagined our arrival in the house as a starting point toward broader and more promising horizons. As if it was only then and there that our adult life was going to take on its proper dimensions. Even though he was forty-one and I was thirty-six. I guess we didn't move very fast. Well, not always.

THE FIRST TRAFFIC LIGHTS were pivoting gas lanterns operated by a police constable in London in 1868 to control traffic on Bridge Street outside the Houses of Parliament. I don't know how modern traffic lights work, but I assume engineers adjust them according to the flow of traffic, so that everything works in the most fluid manner possible. When I'm at the wheel of my car, I try to go at just the right speed to catch several green lights in a row. Sometimes I slow down so I can feel the pleasure of seeing the lights in front of me turning green one after another, like a red carpet unfolding before me, if I can put it that way, thereby creating complete harmony between humans (me) and machines lodged in electronic boxes. There's no use going too fast. It's best just to wait for the mysterious pleasure of the road opening before you.

I think I got obsessed with traffic lights because the tendency today is toward roundabouts (admittedly more in the countryside than in the city). It's as if it were no longer allowed to put a stop to flows, people, fluids, the workings of time; it's as if modern man, no longer able to tolerate any interruption of his drives and impulses, had begun to imitate the communication that flows night and day through the always-open valves of networks. From this standpoint, traffic lights must seem like reactionary beings that forbid unlimited entry and force us to bang our heads against closed doors. A little like a closed border, a categorical refusal. The free movement of trade, of commodities (this is the whole problem), of currencies, and of ideologies has rendered the very notion of red lights obsolete. But I digress.

SO WHEN THE LIGHT in front of the Musée Guimet turned yellow, Claude was tempted to speed right through it, even though he was still a block away, even though he wasn't expecting the interruption, because everything to that point had been as smooth as velvet, he hadn't even had to stop near the Brasserie des Brotteaux or the Clinique du Parc (which has since moved). After all, he wouldn't have put anyone in danger, since as far as he could see there weren't any cars waiting on the rue Boileau, which ran perpendicular. He hesitated for a fraction of a second, undoubtedly trying his best to behave, because he still had the sweet taste of his morning transgression running through his veins. *Should I try to make it or not? Either way, I have to do something. Either I accelerate (at the risk of smashing into the car in front of me) or I brake (at the risk of being hit from behind).* And at the very last moment, he bowed to the authority of the law. I can see him getting just the slightest bit annoyed, quietly swearing through his teeth in anticipation of the comedown that would ensue as he shifted to a lower gear, the pleasure that would vanish as he slowed down, making way for the frustration of the one who gives in, who throws in the towel. The one who finds himself in the same situation as the people sitting in their cars all around him. All of them stopped at the starting line. All of them castrated—we might as well say it. All falling behind the schedule they'd set for themselves.

Back then no one had a cell phone to set down on his lap, to look at whenever there was a pause in the action, a snag in traffic; all we had to get us through the wait was our patience, a radio we could fiddle with, and visors we could pull down to fix a loose strand of hair. For bikers, all there was to do during those thirty seconds of forced immobility was look at a girl passing by, make sure your backpack was attached properly, and check your watch to make sure you weren't late. Sometimes today when I'm driving I come upon a biker checking his phone, and I feel a certain tenderness as I watch him trying to tap the screen with gloved fingers.

AND IT HAS TO be said that stopping at a red light has become even worse now that poor people, homeless people, and refugees ask us for money through the window, try to sell us a newspaper that might allow them to stay afloat, ask for change that may end up in someone else's hands. We think of them as something we have to put up with, or even as a new kind of toll booth. Claude often said that they never approach bikers, that they see them as a different species, a kind of mystery beneath gear that makes them unapproachable, thereby turning them into scarecrows. After all, would it make any sense to engage a deep-sea diver in conversation? A beekeeper? An astronaut on his way to the moon? They imagine bikers as having no face, no voice, and no wallet.

CLAUDE STOPPED, NORMALLY, CAREFULLY, in front of the Musée Guimet, which at that point was a natural history museum, in pole position, ready to set off again. He turned his head to the left and saw teenagers coming out of the museum, hurried along by their teacher. We'd often visited the museum on Sundays in winter with our child, keen to expose him to everything that was most captivating in the natural world, to those plates containing beetles, butterflies, and every imaginable kind of insect on the top floor in a glass cabinet, the skeleton of a giant killer whale (our son informed us that it was the most fearsome of all sea predators, and that its name was *Orcinus orca*, the one who brings death), stuffed antelopes and a stuffed wolf, Egyptian mummies in the basement, and the Asian masks that Émile Guimet no doubt brought back from his trips to the Far East, which was the specialty of this industrialist and great collector from Lyon, who was born in 1836, on June 2 (which meant he had the same birthday as Claude—it's a silly detail, but I'm trying to find meaning in every detail), and who contributed to the creation of the museum, which was one of the most peaceful and elegant places in the city. It has since closed, and its collections have been transferred to the Musée des Confluences, in an attempt to make them appear less outdated.

Claude didn't know any of this, but I'd have to make a long list if I wanted to write down everything he didn't know about the world that has kept turning without him.

WHEN CLAUDE LOOKED TOWARD the entrance to the museum where the students were gathered, he may simply have thought of the subdued light that prevailed inside the building, or the huge mammoth skeleton that takes up the entire ground floor, or his junior high school days in Rillieux-la-Pape, being hurried along by his teachers in the staircases of the school rather than the museum, because no one thought to bring children to the museum in our generation.

What do I really know about his final thoughts as he sat there, brought to a halt by the red light that would bring his life to a halt, in front of a group of teenagers excited about their pending vacations? What went through his mind at 4:24 p.m. on that Tuesday, June 22, at the very end of the twentieth century?

Did he hum a tune, repeating those three notes from "Dirge" by Death in Vegas that may have been stuck in his head? Or was he actually singing "I Wanna Be Your Dog" by the Stooges, one of those cult songs that he whistled sometimes at the kitchen table while clinking on a bottle with a knife, to create the broken glass effect that Iggy Pop used to establish a rhythm? This amused our son, who also wanted to clink his knife, and Claude let him tap out a few bars, keen to hand down an inheritance in rock and roll in addition to his formal education.

Claude waited for the light to turn green so he could ride for about three more blocks down the final straight stretch of road before the Rhône, then cross the Pont de la Boucle and climb up toward the school on the rue Eugène-

Pons, which people in the Croix-Rousse district know well for its narrowness, the walls of its silk workshops, the traffic jam every morning between eight and nine fifteen in the downhill direction, the primary school halfway up the slope, just before the turn, the woman in the fluorescent vest who helps the kids to cross (the kids call her "the crossing lady"), the parents who gather in front of the school gate, and the groups of children who make motorists panic.

Claude waited, no more than five minutes from the school. Maybe he looked at the passenger in the car beside him, who was checking the mirror to see if her lipstick needed a touch-up. But actually I imagine him sitting about three feet ahead of her, both feet fastened solidly to the ground, his long legs steady on each side of the bike, ready to shift into first with his left foot, to press down on the shifter and activate the transmission with a click, and at the same time to disengage the clutch with his left hand, before turning the throttle and liberating himself from the cars at the stop line.

Claude waited, and I wonder if some secret power, some invisible force, could have prevented him from setting off, made him stay where he was, kept him from rushing headlong into the danger that was waiting for him about a block up the road.

DON'T MOVE.

DON'T PLAY THAT GAME the traffic light forces you into by deciding when you stop and when you start. Just stay there and watch the students horsing around on the steps of the museum. Just stay there, linger, get lost in whatever thoughts come into your mind, thoughts that bring you back to your housing development, to the class where you sat beside Mohamed Amini, who would become the guitarist of the group Carte de Séjour, "Residence Permit," and who would invite you to your first rock concerts. Mohamed Amini, who has just died at the moment I'm writing these lines, like your friend Rachid Taha, the group's singer, who was born in Algeria the same year as you.

JUST STAY RIGHT THERE. Don't move.

"SHOULD I STAY OR should I go?" as Joe Strummer, lead singer of the Clash, sang on the album *Combat Rock* in 1982. Which Claude knew by heart, and which he danced to from time to time, in that way he had of moving his feline body, putting his arms forward and then his legs (always hugged by tight pants) in a nod to his new-wave days.

IF ONLY I HADN'T gone to Paris on Tuesday, June 22, but Friday, June 18, as planned. If only my brother hadn't needed a garage. If only the Merciers hadn't ceded to my desire to buy their house. If only we hadn't gotten the keys in advance. If only my mother hadn't called my brother. If only I hadn't declined my brother's proposal to bring our son on holiday. If only I'd phoned from Paris to tell Claude not to go pick our son up at school. If only Claude hadn't taken my brother's bike. If only he hadn't left his three hundred francs in the cash machine. If only he'd listened to Coldplay and not Death in Vegas. If only Tadao Baba hadn't existed. If only the free trade agreements between Japan and the European Union hadn't been signed. If only it hadn't been so nice that day. If only Denis R. hadn't brought his Citroën 2CV to his father. If only the light hadn't turned red. If only, if only, if only, if only, if only, if only, if only.

OBVIOUSLY, CLAUDE SET OFF when the light turned green.

HE SHIFTED INTO FIRST. The witnesses didn't see anything (why doesn't anyone ever see anything? What do they do with their eyes when they're out walking?), but they heard the loud noise of an acceleration. The police report, which I'm holding in my hands, is unequivocal. Claude set off like a shot. As if he'd been riding in the famous Japanese race for which the bike was designed, the Suzuka 8 Hours. Even though in an endurance race you probably don't need to set off like a house on fire. Strange expression. It probably led to the bike popping a wheelie. No one saw anything, but everyone heard it.

NOR WAS CLAUDE DEAF to this loud sound he produced, probably in spite of himself. He wasn't deaf, but he'd been suffering from tinnitus for a few years, probably the result of constantly listening to music at a very high volume, especially in concert halls, where decibel levels weren't really regulated in the early eighties, which is when he began to go to a lot of concerts. The tinnitus usually bothered him at night, when all the noise outside of him had stopped, which allowed him to hear a kind of inner blowing, creating a din that bothered him so much that he sometimes had to get up and walk around the apartment until the sound frequencies agreed to leave his skull.

Today I think I can safely say that Claude didn't mean to pop a wheelie, the famous wheelie riders mention on the sites I've looked at, when the bike's front wheel comes off the ground due to an imbalance between the bike's very light weight and its enormous power.

Claude accelerated just a bit too quickly, making the Honda CBR900 rear up in spite of itself and throw its rider onto the road, right in front of the five-star Hôtel Reine Astrid, the Queen Astrid, named after that goddess who'd come from a northern land she'd never see again, who was queen of Belgium until a car accident cost her her life in 1935, when she was barely thirty years old, driving with her husband, King Léopold III, in a Bugatti convertible near Lake Lucerne in Switzerland.

YOU CAN LOOK FOR every possible coincidence, every imaginable sign, in the interconnections between events, occurrences, dates. You can look at how Belgium, Japan, and Algeria met up tragically on the asphalt of Lyon. You can go on and on about it, you can look for meaning where there isn't any. But knowing that Claude fell in front of the Hôtel Reine Astrid, or, let's just say it, at the feet of Queen Astrid, I know it sounds stupid, but knowing this makes his death a bit less painful, because it's as if he'd gone to join the queen in her grave. As if there was a secret connection between everyone who died in road accidents. Which puts to bed once and for all the idea of an isolated death, or a death that happens by chance, what we call an accidental death, which we place in the category of human interest stories, miscellaneous news items, as opposed to those more respectable deaths, those collective deaths that belong to great historical movements. Slipping on a banana peel isn't the same as being rounded up and killed by a dictator. That's why I'm looking for partners, as it were, people whose deaths remind me of Claude's death. And also why I'm looking for patterns where there don't appear to be any, patterns that are sociological or political, even though I may be fantasizing or embellishing them. Because in truth there's no reason for any of this.

KNOWING THAT ASTRID'S HUSBAND, who was at the wheel, swerved as he was glancing at a road map that his wife was having trouble deciphering, and then crashed into a tree before ending his race in the reeds of the lake, reassures me in a way, but also perplexes me. And allows me to observe that cars and motorcycles have nothing in common where the passenger is concerned. The passenger is never the one who reads the map on a bike. She doesn't really participate, in fact she's kind of irrelevant, she can't give any advice because of the wind and the noise of the engine, she can't give those awkward warnings that in a car would lead to arguments and even threats, especially the

threat that consists of saying: "Stop the car and let me out."
It's totally different for a couple on a motorcycle because
you can't share any words, all you can do is hold on and let
yourself be carried along as you try to be as light as possible. Of course, you can always sit there shaking in silence,
and you can always make a scene once the ride is over.

IF I'D BEEN A passenger on June 22, 1999, the accident
wouldn't have happened. But actually I couldn't have
been a passenger, because there's not enough room
for two people on the Honda CBR900. Well, if you look
closely, there's a tiny cushion above the shock absorber,
but I'd never have agreed to sit on it because it would be
degrading—I'd look like a frog. Which would contradict
the relaxed attitude that's part of the pleasure of riding
a motorbike, whether as a driver or a passenger, like on
Claude's Suzuki Savage, designed to look like a less flashy
version of the bikes from *Easy Rider*, the Dennis Hopper
film that resulted in hordes of clones flooding the streets,
ridden by people trying to relive the American dream,
back when it still meant something.

THE TIME OF THE accident written in the police report is
4:25 p.m. The place: the corner of the boulevard des Belges
and the rue Félix-Jacquier. Félix Jacquier, at once famous
and unknown, if I can put it that way, had the distinction
of being one of the city's first bankers, and he was also
the president of Lyon's public hospitals from 1858 to 1867.
Which means that, without realizing it, he was part of the

welcome party for Claude when he arrived at the emergency room. Damn, this city's like a well-oiled machine.

Claude fell at the feet of a queen and into the hands of a banker. In different parts of the city, which complicates things, because the neighborhoods of Lyon all tell different stories. Claude lived on the *colline des canuts*, hill of the silk workshops, where in 1831 (at the very moment France was colonizing Algeria) the workers started an insurrection that then spilled over into the posh neighborhoods. I'm doing the best I can to locate a symbol in this ridiculous jumble, but all I find, to my great disappointment, are absurdities. There's nothing to understand, nothing to see—it's like trying to wring out a dry cloth.

And yet.

23

If only Denis R. hadn't decided to bring the Citroën 2CV to his father

AT THE MOMENT CLAUDE WAS LEAVING THE LIBRARY, the driver of the Citroën, Denis R., who would arrive from the opposite direction, and whose name would be written on the police report, must have also been leaving his place of work, a primary school where he was a student teacher. This young man of twenty-three, who is in no way responsible for the accident, was arriving at low speed at the moment Claude fell and then slid across the roadway.

AT THE MOMENT CLAUDE was leaving the library, Denis R. was getting into the Citroën that belonged to his father, bringing it back to him so that it could be scrapped. This was the final ride for this car that had come to the end of the line. Denis R. shouldn't have been driving down that boulevard on that day, because he was planning to bring the car back on the weekend, but he changed his mind at the last minute and decided to drive it over when he left work. Best to take care of it now, he must have thought, then I'll be done with it. That's what he told me when we met several years later.

His dad's car, my brother's bike.

I'D LATER LEARN THAT Denis R. is a musician, that he likes the same music Claude did, that he started a band and recorded an album. When I finally felt ready to write to him, and then to meet him, almost ten years later, I first went to see him in concert, perhaps just to tell myself: "That's him," to look at those eyes that saw what I have no knowledge of. At first he covered some songs by Mathieu Boogaerts, whom Claude had interviewed a few months before the accident, I remember perfectly because afterward he'd brought me that canary-yellow promo T-shirt in which I slept for years (and which I've kept even though it's completely faded), and on which the name of one of Boogaerts's albums, *Super!*, is written.

So Denis R. started with some Mathieu Boogaerts, the concert was at the Marché Gare in Lyon, a concert hall that was in bad shape but has now been renovated, in the middle of a huge building site that has disfigured the La Confluence neighborhood. I asked Marie to come with me, since I was thinking I'd go see Denis R. in his dressing room after the show, which I fortunately didn't have the courage to do.

Since the accident, Denis R. has recorded several rather

melancholic albums, including one that contains a song called "Sorry." Which obviously isn't related, but I've decided it is. You can make song lyrics say anything you want. Just like you can find meaning in any form of reality.

The twenty-three-year-old who was driving the Citroën and the one who performed first aid are the same man. Because in addition to being a teacher and a musician, he was a volunteer fireman. It's also what he would tell me that day we met in a café in the Croix-Rousse. He would tell me the last words Claude ever spoke.

I CAME BACK FROM Paris on the TGV that got into Lyon at nine o'clock, and I didn't have to run to catch the train because it hadn't taken me much time to see the Ousmane Sow installation at the Pont des Arts. I even decided to walk to the Gare de Lyon, to make the most of the warm air and think about all the great things that had happened that day. When the train pulled in, Guy was waiting for me at the end of the platform. He'd been informed of the accident but didn't have many details. He just told me it was a shoulder injury. I was surprised to see him, but not that surprised. I didn't think to ask him how he'd found out. From that point on we were in action mode. Guy said he wanted to drop me off at home, but once we got there, he stayed. He paced back and forth in the living room, which was filled with boxes, as I listened to the messages on the answering machine. There was nothing out of the ordinary, just a message from Christine, Louis's mom, who'd asked our son to sleep over at their place after the birthday party. And two missed calls. Guy turned down the beer I offered him.

Guy was acting strange, but I didn't notice. Everything seemed off-kilter, but it didn't bother me. My brain had no doubt already been affected and was starting to push the denial button. Guy suggested we go to the hospital to get some news. He couldn't stop moving. Yes, of course, we had to be there. Guy drove through Lyon's deserted streets. He smoked with the window open, offered me cigarettes, I smoked with him in the warm evening air. It wasn't night yet, the day was stretching out, and I had no idea what was happening. I was still in the aura of that day in Paris, where I'd received so many good signals about my novel that would soon be published, and I was filled with anticipation for the coming literary season. I had a book for Claude in my bag, which I'd slipped into a nice envelope. The book was called *Nico*, and he would never read it.

When we got to the Édouard-Herriot Hospital, Guy gave his name at reception, but it was too soon to give him any information. I waited in the car, and I wasn't really worried yet. Guy was nervous and quiet, but he's always been like that, even during the weekends we often used to spend together, along with Michelle, Philippe, and Béatrice, on land a farmer lent him in the region of Bresse. We went back to the apartment, and I checked the answering machine again, but there was still no news. Guy again turned down the beer I offered, saying he wanted to make a call. When he hung up, he said it was serious. I didn't dare ask. Probably I didn't want to know. Guy was frowning, but he often frowns, even when we go pick mushrooms in a field, even when he lights the fire in a wood stove. I got back in the car and let him drive me. I let him take charge. We rode, and I remember it taking a long time.

Toward midnight, after he'd inquired again at reception, Guy came and asked me to get out of the car. I had the feeling my sandals were a bit too big, I'd have to adjust the strap. I did what he asked. After a moment's hesitation, during which he seemed to fade in and out, a woman spoke to me in the parking lot. I don't know where she came from. It was dark all around. I didn't realize she was an emergency doctor. She's the one who said the words that cut my life in two: "There was nothing we could do." The words that divide a before from an after. The fold that's as sharp as a blade. Everything around us had disappeared—there was nothing but her face in the night. A face I wouldn't recognize today.

IT TOOK ME WEEKS to find out Claude's time of death. Nine thirty p.m. The hospital gave me the runaround, transferring me from one department to another whenever I phoned. They asked me once why I needed "that piece of information." Because deep down I knew, intuitively I knew, but I wanted to be sure, I wanted them to tell me. He'd waited for me.

LATER I'D LEARN THAT the emergency doctor in the parking lot was also the wife of the notary, the friend of Claude who was so accommodating. And here again there's nothing more to say, nothing to understand, it's just chance. A simple choreographic movement.

Encounters, friendships, misunderstandings, favors. Weekends in the country. Coincidences. Life in all its fluidity.

THERE'S NOTHING TO UNDERSTAND. Everyone plays his role. Everyone has his proper place in the city: doctor, notary, teacher, fireman, police officer, librarian, banker, priest. Everyone has the right to be there. That's what society's all about.

It's a well-oiled machine. It works, and then sometimes it stops working, for better or for worse.

Journalist, undertaker, writer.

There's no such thing as "if only."

The Eclipse

EVERYONE WAS TALKING ABOUT THE ECLIPSE. YOU could never have imagined it—everyone was looking for glasses you could use to look at the sun that was supposed to disappear behind the moon in the middle of the day. Actually you could find these glasses anywhere, at the tobacconist's, at the pharmacy, in market stalls. Glasses that were approved and others, counterfeit ones, that you had to steer clear of if you didn't want to burn your retinas. The eclipse was during the last summer of the century. It was summer one last time, and for the first time it was summer without you.

PACO RABANNE PREDICTED THAT the world would end with the *Mir* space station crashing over Paris, and I was grateful to him for coming up with a piece of news that I cared about. I wanted to believe him, I wanted to think he was right, that we'd all be cut down, all of us equally, but I couldn't confide this awful thought to anyone.

ON AUGUST 11, I didn't have any plans, no more than August 10 or August 12—my week was desperately empty. The stretch of time I was in felt like a vast wasteland. It was during the two weeks when Théo was at summer camp. I was wondering if I shouldn't actually cancel his trip to the countryside, but I was afraid that doing so would simply add disorder to madness. This is what our life had become. What would you have done in my place? There were valid reasons for each option, and it was hard for me to think clearly, since the person I'd normally discuss it with was gone. I decided I wouldn't change the plan, since we'd spent a lot of time deciding on it. I slipped the glasses for the eclipse into Théo's bag. At least that would give him something to talk about, because we'd been left without words by the enormity of what had happened.

Maybe he'd think of me as he watched the eclipse, since I'd be looking at the same thing as him. We'd be joined by the same moment, lost in the heart of the solar system.

He'd no doubt think of you, his star that was disappearing behind the moon.

I woke up so late that the sun was already high in the sky. The eclipse would take place at 11:22 a.m. I needed that number 22, which kept coming up. I started the car after taking a ridiculously long shower. I covered the miles separating me from my parents' house without turning on the radio (I couldn't listen to music anymore—I understood Marguerite Duras, who'd talked about how music could devastate her, which to that point I'd thought of as a bit precious). The highway, vacationers towing their speed-boats, couples with their children, life flowing like warm water from a tap.

The lives of others.

I was thirty-six, and I was going to my parents' place to watch the eclipse. I hoped Paco Rabanne was right.

He was a strange one, that Paco whom I suddenly liked so much, he'd also lost his dad when he was young, he'd been shot by Franco, and I told myself that if Paco Rabanne got over it, Théo would too, I was thinking by free association, thoughts were coming to me any old way, a father shot and twenty years later, his child, now an adult, put together a fashion show with twelve "unwearable" dresses made of metal, glass, and leather, which revolutionized our aesthetic notions, because the child who had now become a fashion designer was the first to hire Black women as runway models. He annoyed the whole world, this Paco, who had his first out-of-body experiences at the age of seven, going on astral voyages in which he lived other lives, extravagant lives, lives different from the one that landed him in the Argelès internment camp with his psychic mother and the ghost of his absent father.

Everyone was making fun of Paco Rabanne that summer, and you could see why people would want to make him look ridiculous, this guy who claimed his ancestors had come to the Basque Country from Atlantis, this guy who said Paris would be destroyed and the world would end because Nostradamus had predicted it, this guy who declared that 1999 would be the year of the great explosion. There were plenty of people who didn't like his prophecies at all, not one bit.

Whereas for me, it liberated me. Sitting there at the steering wheel, I was praying that at 11:22 the sky would cloud over, and then gradually become more threatening until it was devoured by darkness, followed by a blaze that would engulf the earth in flames. The only thing I'd have asked for would be to have Théo pressed against me.

MY DAD RAN OUT to the gate, alerted by the noise of my Peugeot 106. He checked his watch and told me to hurry. There'd be no time to plop down in an armchair and have coffee, no time to ask each other how we were doing, which in any case would have been beyond us at that point. He gave us our glasses (they'd been included with his newspaper subscription) and had us stand on the patio, my mother on one side and me on the other. We looked like an Edward Hopper painting, standing immobile before the landscape, a little stiff and ill at ease while we waited for the show to start. I hadn't glanced at the horizon since the day of the accident, because I was terrified of all the beauty that had become inaccessible to me. (My cousin had brought me to Giverny in July to breathe some life into me, and I tried to appreciate the water lilies and all that, but I was still in complete denial, seeing the world through a pane of glass, it was the beginning of a long journey in which I felt like I was traveling alongside myself.)

Maybe you were in the sky after all, like Aunt Olivia told Théo on the day of your funeral. ("Your dad's going up to the sky," this is the kind of thing Théo had to put up with, while for me it was "What doesn't kill you makes you stronger.") I stared at the sky for longer than I should have, and thankfully my cardboard glasses protected me.

The neighbors, standing in their garden, waved to my parents. A gulp of swallows plunged steeply and then disappeared. A dog's barking slowly became a soft whining. Everything got quiet. Everything was heavy, worrisome. The heat of the patio ebbed and the shadow started spreading. I felt the air turn cold, as if the blood was draining out of my veins and my entire body.

THIS IS ALL TWENTY years ago now. It's time for me to lay down my arms and stop fighting. Leaving the house means letting go of you.

The nature all around me will soon turn to concrete and the landscape will disappear. Just like the sound of your voice disappears sometimes.

It's been such a long journey.

All these insane years since your fall. During which I also fell, in every conceivable way. And got back up again. And kept seeing you when I wasn't looking for you. There were so many signs, so many coincidences, so many secret encounters. That whole ineffable part of life. I felt like I was melting into you, like I was both a man and a woman.

AND EVERYTHING THAT HAPPENED. The friends who helped me repaint the house and who formed a protective barrier around me. The books I wrote, their words like bricks I had to lay in spite of everything. Théo and his inventiveness, his ideas for bringing you back to life and saving us. The birthday when I turned forty and danced in front of everybody. And new things as well, the feeling of danger that accompanied them and gradually faded away, and the subsequent freedom—unexpected, terrifying— that made me take risks. The giddiness of falling in love again, even though I still missed you. Desire and sorrow mixed together, every possible contradiction, life swirling around like a washing machine.

 · Faithfulness and guilt.

All the big words.

A sort of double life, throbbing and pulsating like a song by Sparks.

NOW I HAVE TO pack my boxes once more, protect your records, wrap up your instruments.

The song of birds will soon be drowned out by the noise of motors. Carburetors yet again. Bulldozers that will flatten everything that was once alive. It's been twenty years, and my memory is full of holes. Sometimes I lose you, sometimes I let you escape from me.

SOMETIMES I HAVE TO concentrate to see your face. That's something I'd never have imagined. To really make out all of its details. I have to summon up one very specific scene to capture your look. I'm not talking about your eyes, whose velvety black intensity I know by heart, but the way you looked at me. I have to focus and re-create a moment that I photographed in my mind. I remember what I said to myself in that moment: If ever anything should happen.

If ever.

I think we all do that. We all try to freeze an image in our minds. If ever.

It was in the apartment, a few weeks before the move. You were crouched over in the bathroom, looking for something in the shelves under the sink, no doubt that gel whose smell I loved, which you used to tame your thick hair. I walked in and you jumped. As if you were annoyed at me for walking in unannounced. I was surprised to find you there, naked from the waist up, almost helpless. You looked up at me. The light was coming in behind you, from the half-open window. You were so handsome.

There was something fragile and touching in the way you looked at me. As if you were arriving from somewhere else. You down near the ground, me standing over you. And your shoulders, your almost adolescent biceps. I mumbled a few words before closing the door; "Sorry" was one of them, but it was a complicit "Sorry," like we were in on something together. You looked at me with false modesty, with the hint of a knowing smile. I held on to that look, that insinuation that spoke volumes, as I backed into the hallway.

I also held on to your intonation, because just before I closed the door, you asked me: "Is everything OK?" That's all you said: "Is everything OK?" In that serious and slightly gravelly voice, as if you wanted to make sure nothing had come between us.

I turned away. Something had happened.

Something that comforted me.